The raging riv
nearly their undoing

Choking, coughing, shivering, Rylla scrambled up the muddy incline.

"We must find shelter and dry out," Jacques said.

Dimly she was aware of being swung aloft before everything became a blur. Propped against a rough, hard surface, she came to, and panicked. "Jacques?"

"I'm here," he answered. "Take off those wet clothes." He handed her the towel from his waterproof knapsack.

Within minutes he had a fire burning and he began to strip off his own clothes. "I have put the sleeping bag near the fire. Please get into it." She did as he asked and was horrified when a moment later he began to scramble in beside her.

"What are you doing?" she squeaked.

"Perhaps you didn't realize, *ma chérie*," he said, "but this is the only protection we have. This, and each other's warmth."

Annabel Murray has pursued many hobbies. She helped found an arts group in Liverpool, England, where she lives with her husband and two daughters. She loves drama: she appeared in many stage productions and went on to write an award-winning historical play. She uses all her experiences—holidays being no exception—to flesh out her characters' backgrounds and create believable settings for her romance novels.

Books by Annabel Murray

Don't miss any of our special offers. Write to us at the following address for information on our newest releases.

Harlequin Reader Service
901 Fuhrmann Blvd., P.O. Box 1397, Buffalo, NY 14240
Canadian address: P.O. Box 603,
Fort Erie, Ont. L2A 5X3

Heart's Treasure

Annabel Murray

Harlequin Books

TORONTO • NEW YORK • LONDON
AMSTERDAM • PARIS • SYDNEY • HAMBURG
STOCKHOLM • ATHENS • TOKYO • MILAN

Original hardcover edition published in 1988
by Mills & Boon Limited

ISBN 0-373-02932-2

Harlequin Romance first edition September 1988

For Alma, who went
to Machu Picchu

CHAPTER ONE

'RYLLA! Rylla! Wake up! We're almost there! You're a fine travelling companion!'

Long, dark lashes fluttered as their owner sought to keep a hold on sleep. Then, unwillingly, brown eyes opened. With a feline luxuriance Rylla Quarmby stretched her long, graceful body. She yawned, groaned a little. But then a familiar sense of excitement, which even a life of constant travel could not dull, banished her fatigue. She sat erect to look out of the aircraft window at the scene below.

She was pleased to see that the sky was clear over Lima. She had visited Peru once before at this time of the year. But then the Garúa, a low, heavy mist, had hung over the capital, shrouding it from view. Today it was possible to get some perspective on the city crowded into the mouth of a river valley. Low sandy mountains enclosed its outer fringes. She turned to her younger brother.

'I'm sorry, Andy. I must have slept for hours. But I needed it. I got into Amsterdam just in time to connect with this flight. I was totally jet-lagged.' She yawned again and pushed back the cloud of long, dark hair which her restless sleep had dishevelled. She grimaced as she looked at the creases in her once-smart cream linen pant-suit. 'I must look a mess.'

'No more than usual,' was her brother's grinning retort. Though he would never have admitted it to her face, he envied Rylla her dark good looks, the high cheekbones and slanted eyes she had inherited from their mother. He had to be content with his father's short, stocky build and pale blue eyes. Andy's blond choirboy-style hair and innocent cherubic countenance belied his twenty-four years and mischievous, sometimes malicious nature. 'How was the trip to Japan, Sis? You fell asleep before I had a chance to ask you.'

'Very successful. I think the magazine editor will be pleased. If so, it may mean a trip to China next year. Oh, Andy, you should see the temples in Japan, and the gardens! Everything is so colourful. I love going to new and exotic places, seeing ancient cultures. I haven't seen the results of my photos, of course. I had to send the films back to my lab in London. I'd have preferred to process them myself. But then I got the wire from Dad saying the usual photographer had let Irving down.'

From her childhood days, Rylla Quarmby had had a passion for photography, which her family had encouraged. And from a hobby it had developed, via a course in photo-journalism, into a worthwhile and lucrative career. Now her free-lance photography work took her all over the world. Her trip to Japan had been on behalf of the glossy *Far Views* magazine. Since she was her own boss, she was free to accept or reject any assignments, but she had jumped at this present trip to South America.

'Of course it had nothing to do with the fact that you couldn't resist another visit to Peru,' Andy teased.

'That, too,' she admitted. 'But mostly because I haven't seen much of Dad this last year. It'll be great to work with him and Irving again. And you, of course, Andy,' she added hastily as his freckled face puckered in mock indignation.

'I'd expected Dad and Irving to be with you,' Rylla commented as their flight touched down on the main runway.

'That was the original idea. But a few days ago Irving suddenly said he was going on ahead. He left me a mountain of paperwork to clear up all by myself,' Andy added indignantly.

'That's what junior assistants are for, isn't it?' his sister teased him, rumpling his hair with an affectionate hand.

'Cheek!' Andy retorted. 'But seriously, Sis, Irving seemed a bit put out about something. He said there'd been a last-minute hitch. D'you suppose he's having problems with the Peruvian Government?'

'I shouldn't have thought so,' Rylla said. 'Irving and Dad are both well known to the officials. They're usually most co-operative about their expeditions.'

'I shouldn't think it's financial, either,' Andy said with undisguised envy. 'Old Irving's filthy rich. Still, even rich men can suffer reverses. He might have decided he wants additional backing. This is going to be a more ambitious project than usual.'

'What about Dad? Did he fly out with Irving?'

'No, and that's another odd thing. You'd think the aged parent would have jumped at it. An extra few days in his beloved Peru! I don't suppose he'll be far behind us.'

For Matthew Quarmby, Peru had been a lifelong obsession. Some people might say it had been a life-time love affair, since he had also taken a beautiful Peruvian as his wife.

'While on the subject of the aged "P",' Andy went on, as they waited to go through passport and Customs checks, 'you don't think he's going a bit ga-ga in his old age? That he's taking us on a wild-goose chase? This most recent theory of his is against all the historical evidence. And I'd hate that French fellow Fresnay to have the last laugh on him.'

Rylla knew she was the only person to whom Andrew would have expressed such doubts. He was fanatically loyal to the father they both adored but also held in awe.

'It's not against the evidence, not now,' she disagreed. 'When did you last see Dad?'

'Two or three months ago. Irving and I only got back from his latest lecture tour last week.'

'I meant to give you Dad's most recent letter to read.' Rylla opened the small holdall she carried as hand luggage. Her wide, generous mouth parted in a rueful smile. 'But I blanked out first.'

Brother and sister boarded the airport bus that was to take them to their hotel in downtown Lima. The vehicle was crammed with laughing, chattering, pointing tourists, but Rylla and Andy took little notice of their surroundings as they pored over their father's spidery handwriting. Rylla indicated the relevant paragraphs.

'He says the document he's been translating is almost certainly genuine. It was only a photostat, of course. The museum at Arequipa wouldn't let the original out of their hands.'

Andy screwed up his eyes and peered closer.

'This fifteenth-century Spaniard, Molina, actually claims to know the whereabouts of the Supreme Inca's treasure?'

'Yes. The Inca king, Atahualpa, despatched some of his wealth inland so Pizarro couldn't get his hands on all of it.'

'We already know that. Explorers have been looking for the lost city and Inca treasure for hundreds of years.' Despite his words, Rylla knew Andy was anxious to be convinced.

'Yes, but perhaps they've been looking in the wrong place.' Rylla's lovely face was flushed with enthusiasm. 'We know the existing maps of the Camino Incaico, the Royal Road, aren't necessarily accurate. Dad says the manuscript mentions a city in the jungle. He believes if we can pick up a missing section of road it will lead us to the city.'

'I hope he's right, especially if there's treasure to be found.' There was a light in Andrew's pale blue eyes that his sister didn't like. His longing for riches troubled Rylla sometimes. She knew Irving Wilder paid his young assistant a generous salary. But Andrew's love of fast cars, nightlife, and his endless stream of girlfriends meant he lived right up to his income. She'd had to advance him money several times to settle his debts.

'Dad and Irving aren't treasure hunters,' she reminded him. 'Anything they find has to be handed over to the authorities. You should know that by now.'

'Yes,' Andy sighed. 'But it's all right for some. Irving doesn't need any more money, anyway. And you and Dad seem to manage. But I could use some extra cash. It always seems a waste to me. All those things lying about in museums, gathering dust.'

'I suppose you'd rather they gathered dust in some millionaire's private collection?'

'If the millionare was paying *me* to find them for him, yes.'

'Those sort of things belong to everyone, Andy.'

'All right, all right! I know. Spare me the lecture.'

The elevator whisked them up to the fourteenth floor of the hotel where Irving Wilder had reserved a whole suite of rooms for the members of his expedition.

'By the way,' Andy said, 'I bumped into Colin Philby in London last week.' Colin was Rylla's current boyfriend. 'He wasn't very pleased to hear you were going straight on from Japan.' Andy seemed to derive considerable satisfaction from the fact.

'No,' Rylla said guiltily. 'He wouldn't be. I did write explaining why, but he won't have had my letter yet.'

'He won't understand, anyway. I can't think what you see in that stick-in-the-mud. Has he ever been any further from home than Southend, do you think?'

'Yes,' Rylla laughed, 'but I must admit he isn't keen on travelling. It's the way he's been brought up, I suppose. His parents are the same. It makes you realise how lucky we were in our parents.'

'And do you think if you marry Colin you'll be able to stand it? Living in a three-bedroom semi, with a husband who's a nine-to-five insurance salesman?'

'He's not *just* an insurance salesman,' Rylla protested. 'And if Colin has his way we'll be living in a large *detached* house in the stockbroker belt. Anyway, we're not even engaged yet.'

'But he wants you to marry him?'

'I think so, yes. When he can afford it.'

'You're earning, too,' Andy pointed out.

'Yes, but Colin says that doesn't count. He

thinks a man should be able to support his wife. He's old-fashioned about things like that. Anyway, there's no rush as far as I'm concerned.'

Rylla was very fond of Colin, of course, but secretly she was glad he hadn't actually proposed yet. She worked long hours, her energies totally dedicated to making her name as a professional photographer. She enjoyed her career and the travelling it involved.

'If you marry Colin, he'll try to put a stop to you going abroad,' Andy said, as though he'd read her thoughts.

'By that time, I hope I'll be established enough to work full-time in England. I shan't give up my career just because I'm married.'

Andy grunted disbelievingly. 'I wouldn't rely too much on Colin agreeing to that. He strikes me as the sort to want his wife safely tied to his home and family. I know you, Sis, and you'd be bored out of your mind married to him. How did you ever meet him, for goodness' sake?'

'He sold me an insurance policy for my cameras.' Rylla couldn't help a chuckle at the expression on her brother's face.

'Typical! And what have you got in common? You like dancing, he doesn't. You like the theatre, he doesn't. And does he ever read a book?'

'He's been too busy studying to read anything but text books,' Rylla defended. 'Anyway, married couples don't have to share everything,' she argued.

'No, but they should share *something*. If you marry him,' Andy predicted, 'the odds are you won't like his friends and he won't like yours. He's jealous of Irving, you know,' Andy went on.

'That's ridiculous! There's never been anything between me and Irving.'

'I wish there were,' Andy retorted. 'I can't stand Colin Philby. He's a plump, boring young man, and he'll be a *fat* boring *old* man by the time he's thirty.' Craftily, he added, 'He had the glamorous Gloria with him, by the way.'

'Oh?' Gloria Ray had been Colin's previous girlfriend, and the other girl had made no secret of the fact she wanted him back. 'They do work in the same office,' Rylla pointed out, determined not to give way to jealousy. It was a destructive emotion. Besides, Andy was only trying to cause trouble.

'Pity he ever finished with her. I'd much prefer Irving as a brother-in-law,' Andy said, 'and I know he likes you.'

'Give it a rest, Andy,' Rylla said wearily. Jet-lag was catching up with her again. She felt tired and sticky, but above all extremely hungry. She'd only had time for a snack in Amsterdam between flights and she'd slept through the in-flight catering arrangements. She certainly didn't feel like entering into the usual arguments about her private life. She was very fond of Irving, but she was in love with Colin, she assured herself firmly, and she trusted him. Naturally there were some aspects of their future to be ironed out. Sometimes Colin's provincial outlook, his possessiveness, annoyed her. But no one was perfect.

In spite of the hotel's air conditioning, Lima in early May was hot and humid, and Rylla was glad of the luxury of her own private shower. Such facilities would be few and far between once they set off on their journey into the interior. She knew this wasn't going to be just a glamorous adventure. There would be hardships, danger, possibly. And once in the forest regions there would be uncomfortable tropical conditions to contend with.

Wrapped in a towel, she debated which of her two dresses she should wear. On this kind of expedition, elegance wasn't the first consideration. You brought only what you could carry yourself.

Before going in search of her brother, she automatically checked her appearance. The long bedroom mirror showed her a girl, taller than average, but well proportioned with beautiful curves of hip and swelling breasts. She had decided on the green dress as being more sophisticated for a hotel dinner. It had been quite an expensive buy and she knew it suited her figure and colouring. She had swept her long dark hair up into its usual neat coil at the back of her head. It would be more sensible for her work to have it cut short, she supposed. But that would have horrified not only Colin, but her father. Matthew Quarmby saw in Rylla all the qualities for which he had loved his late wife. Rylla knew she was her father's favourite child, a fact which irked Andrew and often drove him on to compete for Matthew's affection and approval. Though she adored her father, sometimes the responsibility of his love was a heavy one.

A message left at reception told brother and sister that Irving Wilder was expected back for dinner. But, since there was no sign of him in the exotically decorated dining-room, Rylla suggested they order.

'I'm starving, and not even the lurid-looking parrots in those murals, not to mention snakes,' she shuddered, 'are going to put me off.' She detested creepy-crawlies, but snakes were her chief *bête noire*.

'Wait till you see the real thing,' Andy told her, 'and the spiders!'

Rylla proved her point about her appetite by doing more than justice to the delicious *ceviche*, a mixture of prawns, scallops and squid, marinated in lime juice and chilli peppers, served 'raw' with corn, sweet potato and onion.

Andy stubbornly insisted on eating 'European'. 'My stomach likes good plain fare. I don't want to risk upsetting it just before a trip.'

They had ordered coffee by the time Irving appeared. That he was not alone was all Rylla registered at first, as he accorded her a bear-hug and a smacking kiss.

'Rylla, love! Good to see you again! Andy!' He acknowledged his young assistant. 'I'd like you both to meet Jacques.' He introduced the man at his side. 'Jacques Fresnay. You've heard of him, of course.'

Rylla's awed 'of course' was echoed, but in less flattering tones, by Andy.

Jacques Fresnay had a strong, lean but sensual face, framed by unruly flaxen hair, long and curling at his neck. As his eyes met hers, she saw they were of a startling gentian-blue. They flickered over Rylla for what seemed like endless moments, making her feel uncharacteristically self-conscious. She was accustomed to men finding her attractive, but something in that blatantly male assessment brought her chin up, as she made her own cool appraisal of the casually but expensively suited figure.

They shook hands all round, and when it came to her turn she found his hand wide-palmed, long-fingered, his grip strong and insistent. At his touch, quite unexpectedly, frighteningly, through her veins there raced liquid fire. With an utmost exertion of her will-power, she fought back the sensation he'd roused in her, met the widened speculative masculine stare. A polite smile returned his quizzical one.

Yes, she'd certainly heard of the illustrious Frenchman. Weaned and brought up on the history and antiquities of Peru, Rylla and Andy shared their father's enthusiasm. Inevitably

Matthew Quarmby's opinions had coloured theirs.

An article, written the previous year by Matthew, speculating about the lost city of the Incas, had drawn critical fire from a certain Professor Jacques Fresnay. His criticism had inflamed Matthew to the point of apoplexy, and his son and daughter knew he still harboured resentment of the younger man's challenge of his statements. Andrew, who did nothing by halves, was hotly partisan. Rylla was of a more moderate temperament and kept a more open mind. She could sympathise with her father's indignation. She felt certain that, as always, his sometimes almost intuitive theories would be proved correct. But, unlike Andy, she could admit that the Frenchman had a point of view. Matthew's article had presented certain assumptions as facts, and Jacques Fresnay had been perfectly within his rights to query them.

But her own knowledge of the Frenchman went back further than this recent intellectual confrontation. Twelve years ago, when she'd been only sixteen, with her school she had attended a series of Jacques Fresnay's lectures on South America. His singular good looks, his scholarship, his worldwide success, phenomenal for so young a man, had earned him much girlish admiration, including Rylla's. Young and impressionable, she had also found him physically attractive. For a long time she had made him the centre of a romantic fantasy, for he'd been far beyond her reach. And, her senses registered, he was still a most attractive man. With an effort of will she turned her eyes away from his compelling features. She had grown beyond teenage hero-worship.

'Dad not with you?' she asked Irving, conscious, though, that the Frenchman was still watching her.

'No.'

'I do hope he's not going to be late again.' Matthew's absent-mindedness, his dilatory ways, could be very irritating to those of more punctual habits. She indicated the remains of their meal. 'I'm sorry, we started without you. My fault. I hadn't had a square meal since Japan.'

'That's OK, my love,' Irving assured her. 'It's good of you to rush half-way round the world at such short notice.' Irving was a big man, though he was not as tall as the Frenchman. Like Rylla's father, he sported a beard, but he was younger and his was dark and less unruly. 'We're late, anyway. We got held up.'

'Problems?'

'Mmm. With the bus.'

Irving Wilder was a wealthy man. He could and did finance his expeditions from his own pocket. The Quarmbys had known him for years. In fact, Irving had been one of Professor Quarmby's students before Rylla was born. On a previous visit to Peru several years ago, Irving had purchased a reject 'school bus' which he'd had done up and fitted out as transport, storage and living accommodation for use on long trips. There were no bunks, as all the available space was needed for catering and other vital equipment. The members of the party had to use sleeping-bags, sometimes on the floor of the bus or, according to weather and altitude, outside in tents. Between expeditions the vehicle was left in Lima in the charge of a local firm of mechanics.

'I expressly told them I wanted it for the day after tomorrow,' Irving explained. 'But they were trying to tell me they couldn't have it ready in under a week. Good God, they've had it here for the last six months. But I soon sorted them out, didn't I, Jacques?'

'*Mais oui!*' the Frenchman said, but somewhat absently. Disconcertingly, his blue eyes were still studying Rylla's unusual but uniquely lovely features.

'Is that why you came on ahead?' she asked. She wished Jacques Fresnay would pay more attention to the meal before him.

'No. That was something else again.' Irving seemed suddenly uneasy and he plunged into a detailed discussion of their proposed itinerary. 'I hope you won't find it too tedious, Andy,' he said to his young assistant. 'But I want to go over some old ground before we break new. I need to look again at earlier discoveries, in the light of what we believe now about the lost city.'

Rylla was well versed in Peruvian history. She knew that for centuries men had sought for a fabled lost Inca city and its reputedly fabulous wealth.

In 1911, the North American explorer Hiram Bingham had discovered the breathtakingly beautiful Machu Picchu. The white granite citadel was constructed in a terraced saddle between two prominent peaks of the Andes. It was believed to be the last refuge of the Incas following the Spanish conquest. This theory had been discounted in 1964, when Gene Savoy had found another massive complex at Vilcabamba. But present-day experts such as Matthew Quarmby and Irving Wilder believed there was more Inca history to be uncovered. Perhaps, although this was their lowest priority, more treasure to be found.

'So where do we start?' Andy asked.

'With the Nasca Lines.' For the first time, Jacques Fresnay contributed something to the conversation. His gaze moved as if reluctantly from Rylla's face. His strongly accented voice was low and sensually husky. His remark drew curious glances from brother and sister. What had it to do with him?

'The Nasca Lines?' Rylla had heard of these, read about them. But she had never visited the site of one of the greatest mysteries of Peru, the designs drawn across the bleak Pampa de San José. 'But they're pre-Inca,' she objected. 'So they can't possibly . . .'

'*D'accord!*' Again the Frenchman spoke. 'But you must know, M'selle Rylla, the Incas adopted and adapted earlier cultures. Of a certainty, they shared the Nascans' obsession with straight lines and symmetry.'

But Rylla looked at Irving for further explanation. He was the expedition leader.

'Irving? I still don't see what Nasca's got to do with the lost city?'

'Well, as you know, for years Matt and I have been studying old documents, making fresh calculations. We believe now that one or two of the Nasca Lines were *ceques*, sacred pathways, which pointed to holy sites.'

'But to Nascan holy sites, surely?'

'Bear with me a minute. Remember, in the nineteen-sixties, Hawkins computed that some of the *ceques* were originally aligned with the Pleiades and other heavenly bodies?'

'Yes, I remember, but I still don't see what these *ceques* have to do with the lost city.' Rylla's attractive features were flushed and earnest as she leant across the table in an effort to make her point, and now the Frenchman's intent eyes found another target for thoughtfulness, as the V of her dress revealed a tantalising glimpse of generously curving, honey-coloured flesh.

'The best thing is for you to read this.' Irving produced a long, bulky envelope from his pocket, and sorted carefully through its contents. 'I received this a few days ago. It's Matt's translation of the manuscript Pedro sent me.'

The manuscript was the one Irving Wilder had learned about from a Peruvian archivist of his acquaintance, Pedro Garcia. According to the notes attached to the translation, it was Matthew's opinion that the original, if genuine, dated back to the time of Francisco Pizarro, the Spanish conqueror of Peru.

'Dad says this manuscript definitely supports *his* theory about Atahualpa.' She looked at the Frenchman, with a hint of satisfaction in her fine dark eyes. Though she was less resentful than Andrew of the Frenchman's challenge, it was time he realised Matthew Quarmby knew what he was talking about.

She knew, too, that fresh evidence, supported by mathematical calculations, had reinforced Matthew's belief. Now here was this manuscript, written by a Spaniard who alleged he had been captured by the Incas and held prisoner in a fabulous hidden city from which he alone had escaped to tell the story. This could be the final key to the centuries-old mystery. Rylla hoped it was, and that Matthew would be justified. She was prepared to wait and see, but Andrew turned to the Frenchman.

'You don't agree with Dad, do you, Professor Fresnay?' he challenged.

'*Non!* Since you ask. Me, I think ...'

'We all know what you think,' Andy interrupted. 'You made it quite clear in the letter you wrote to the journal.'

'Andy!' Rylla gave a dismayed half-laugh, taken aback by her brother's bluntness, his sudden attack.

'Jacques is entitled to his opinion,' Irving put in.

'Yes.' Rylla was aware she had nonplussed the Frenchman by agreeing. His eyes on her had narrowed considerably. 'He's entitled to his opinion.' But family loyalty made her feel she should support her brother to some extent. 'But surely he should know better than to argue with someone of Dad's knowledge and experience.' Brown eyes challenged the Frenchman's blue ones and there was an odd stillness, a silence which Irving broke impatiently.

'Could we stick to the point? We were discussing Alonso de Molina's manuscript.' His large forefinger tapped the paper Rylla still held. 'If you read on you'll see Molina refers to "sacred lines" and to the lost city as Huacaintiraymi— "Sacred to the Sun". We all know the Incas practised Inti—sun worship. According to Molina, he was lucky to escape with his life, let alone treasure. That treasure may still be there. It's Matt's theory that one of those *ceques* will point straight towards the Sacred City of the Incas. Anyway, it's our only clue at present, so I intend to follow it up.'

'So what then, after Nasca?' Rylla asked.

They had left the restaurant now and were on

their way back to their suite of rooms. She hadn't heard Irving invite Jacques Fresnay to join them, but she supposed he must have done so.

'We'll make our way round to Cuzco and follow the Royal Road north, until it intersects with the bearings I intend to take east from Nasca. Then we'll turn off into the jungle.' Irving sounded confident.

Rylla knew that the Inca Royal Road had been built originally to connect Cuzco in Southern Peru with Quito, the Incas' northern capital, and now the capital of Ecuador.

'Sounds good,' Andy said with a defiant glance at the Frenchman, as they entered the communal lounge of their suite. His comment brought a retort.

'To me, it sounds what you call the "long shot"?'

Irving moved to pour drinks. 'Maybe, Jacques. But sometimes long shots pay off. Think of the results if Matt's right. What have we got to lose?'

'Well, it all sounds pretty exciting to me,' Rylla said, though she could understand the Frenchman's misgivings. 'But where on earth has Dad got to? If he sent you that translation, he obviously hasn't forgotten where he's supposed to be.' Matthew might frequently mislay his pipe or his spectacles. He might even forget his own name one day, his family teased him. But forget anything to do with his lifelong study of Peru? Never! 'I thought he'd be here, just panting to get started.'

'Perhaps, *mon ami*,' Jacques put in suddenly, 'it would be as well now to tell Rylla and Andrew what has happened?'

'Yes, I suppose so.' But Irving sounded reluctant, suddenly tired. 'Rylla,' he handed her the sherry she'd asked for, 'I'm sorry, love. Your father's not making this trip, after all.'

'You're kidding!' was Andy's incredulous reaction.

'What? He's not . . .?' Rylla's hand jerked, and some of the sherry spotted her dress. But she didn't notice, even when Jacques Fresnay proffered his handkerchief. 'Dad always works with you. That's the chief reason I agreed to take this assignment. Because it would mean a chance to work with him. I don't see much of him these days.'

'I know, my dear. But he's decided he's not coming, nevertheless.' Irving felt in his inside pocket. 'He enclosed a letter for the pair of you with mine.'

Rylla almost snatched the envelope from his hand and ripped it open. With Andrew peering over her shoulder she scanned the lines of spidery writing. It didn't take long. Matthew might spend hours on transcribing ancient manuscripts, but his personal correspondence was brief to the point of terseness.

'Dear Rylla and Andrew,' she read. 'I shan't be making this trip. For reasons I won't go into, it seems best all round. Shame I shan't be seeing you, after all, or be "in at the kill". So just remember I'm depending on you two. Last time I saw you, Rylla, you saw fit to imply that I was a pigheaded, obstinate old idiot.'

Shocked, Andy looked up. Though neither of them feared Matthew, his children had always held him in respectful awe. His temper, when lost, was of volcanic proportions. And neither of them would have dreamt of hurting his feelings.

'Rylla, you didn't?'

'No.' Her reading had kept pace with his. 'Well, not exactly. I wouldn't dare. But you know what Dad's like when he gets a bee in his bonnet. Sometimes I think he believes Peru is his exclusive property, that no one else has any right to an opinion.'

Andrew looked at her reprovingly. She knew he didn't like her speaking so frankly before the Frenchman. But, before he could put his reproach into words, '*Eh, bien!* A trait which, it would seem, runs in the family!'

The Frenchman's colloquial English was excellent. His tone was light. But all his efforts gained him was a frosty stare from Rylla's dark eyes. Matthew's family were permitted to criticise him. Strangers were not.

Rylla read on, became thoughtful, heard her brother's sharp intake of breath.

'So it's up to you two to uphold the family honour. I want proof. I know it'll be there. Proof positive, pictorial, if possible, that I'm right about Atahualpa. And the pair of you can tell that damned arrogant Frenchman from me to take his theory about Huascar and . . .' There followed a blunt directive which made Rylla blush and brought a choke of laughter from Andy.

'But it doesn't tell us anything,' Rylla protested when she'd finished reading. 'It doesn't say why he's not coming.'

Respected and famous in his field, Matthew was much in demand as a consultant and as a lecturer. He was always in the midst of writing yet another book or learned paper. But Rylla was almost certain he had no outstanding commitments. It was only a couple of months since she'd seen him. There'd been nothing in the offing then, apart from this trip.

She thought affectionately of their leavetaking. As always, Matthew had been brusquely affectionate, as though ashamed of showing any of the softer emotions.

'Take care, Rylla.' And then, something he rarely did, he'd mentioned her mother. 'You get more like my Santana every day.'

Matthew had adored his beautiful wife. That had been evident to everyone who had seen them together, not least their children. Since Santana had died, Matthew had scarcely spoken her name, as if to do so were too painful to be borne.

'But how will you manage without Dad?'

Irving and Matthew had co-operated for years, and were friends as well as colleagues. Matthew had taught the younger man all he knew. They made a good team, Irving with his sometimes plodding common sense, Matthew with his almost intuitive flair.

'I've invited someone else in his place.'

'Irving!' Rylla cried out in disbelief. 'You're not by any chance telling us this was your idea? I can't believe Dad would change his mind just like that. Who have you asked to replace him, for goodness' sake?' Her tone implied that there was no competent substitute for Matthew Quarmby.

'The only man,' Irving said gravely, 'who is uniquely qualified to do so.'

Incredulously Rylla followed the sideways drift of his eyes. She met the twinkling complacence of gentian-blue ones that seemed already to have gauged her reaction.

'Professor Fresnay?' she said half disbelievingly.

'Oh?' Andy was cynical as he looked at the Frenchman. 'Of course! You're well off, aren't you? Wealthier than Dad will ever be. See, Rylla, I told you Irving might need additional backing this trip!' He added bitterly, 'And, now Fresnay's going to follow up Dad's theory, one on which he's spent most of his life!'

'Dad must have known Professor Fresnay would be replacing him?' Rylla asked. 'He must have known when he wired me?'

'Yes,' Irving said. 'He did. He was afraid you'd refuse to come if you knew he couldn't. But, Rylla, Matthew wants you to make this trip, as much as I do. You're a damned good photographer and, just

as importantly in this case, you know the
background to what you're photographing. Andrew, I think you owe Professor Fresnay an
apology. Don't jump to unjustified conclusions,
either of you. And Rylla, don't make any hasty
decisions. You're tired now, and disappointed
about Matt. We all understand that, eh, Jacques?
But you'll feel differently about it in the morning.'
He rose from his chair yawning hugely. 'Must be
this hot, sticky weather, but I'm whacked. How
about you, Jacques?'

'*Non*. I am not tired yet. I shall take a walk
before retiring. Peru by night is as fascinating as
Peru by day. Would anyone care to accompany
me?' The invitation was made directly to Rylla,
but she shook her head impatiently.

Left alone, brother and sister looked at each
other. Andy stretched out his hand for their
father's letter and read it again.

'You realise what this means, don't you, Sis?' he
asked. 'The aged "P" is as good as ordering us to
carry on his feud with Fresnay for him. Well, I'm
willing to obey orders. I don't care for Fresnay. He
looks the arrogant type. So what are we going to
do about it? We'd better have a plan of campaign.'

'I don't think *you'd* better do anything,' Rylla
said warningly. She knew Andrew could be as pigheaded and belligerent as their father. 'You don't
want to jeopardise your position with Irving, do
you? He obviously thinks well of Jacques Fresnay.' Rylla reflected that she'd never known

Irving Wilder make an error of judgement where character was concerned. He was well aware of Andy's shortcomings, for a start. If the younger man hadn't been Matthew Quarmby's son, he might have been less likely to employ him. 'And as far as I'm concerned it won't be anything so undignified as a feud. Though I shall make it quite clear to him where my loyalties lie. Obviously, we must make sure Dad does get any credit that's coming to him. Andy, why do you think he's not coming? Do you think Irving really did drop him?'

'You'll have to ask him, won't you?' Slyly, 'Maybe if you can get him on his own he'll tell *you*.'

She ignored the implication. She was tired of her brother's continual matchmaking efforts where Irving was concerned. It would suit Andy only too well to have a rich in-law. But, even so, Irving must be pressed for a straight answer. He'd neatly sidestepped the reason for Matthew's absence, neither confirming nor denying Andy's accusation about Jacques. But Rylla felt Andy had hit on the truth. According to rumour, the Frenchman's wealth matched Irving's. He had either bought his way in, or was personally responsible in some other way for Matthew's exclusion.

Even so, she didn't much care for the role her father had allotted his children. She disliked conflict. As yet, the Frenchman had said little, but there had been a certain expression on his face, a certain glint in his blue eyes. And Rylla had a nagging notion that opposing Jacques Fresnay could prove dangerous.

'Strange that Jacques Fresnay hasn't been on television or in the news lately,' Rylla commented, as brother and sister separated to go to their individual rooms. 'At one time he was always in the public eye.'

'Perhaps he's run out of things to discover!' Andy said acidly. 'That's probably why he's got so much time to spend on debunking other people's theories.'

Next morning, as she showered, pulled on working jeans and T-shirt. Rylla considered the best way to approach Irving. She'd been dismayed to hear that her father wasn't coming. But she was a professional. This was her work. It would be most *un*professional to let his absence deter her from what was a lucrative assignment, as well as a potentially exciting one. And for Matthew's sake she ought to be with the expedition if—no, *when* it discovered the lost city. She'd be there to take photos, and to see Jacques Fresnay's face when her father was proved right. She could do that much for Matthew. She didn't want any unpleasantness.

Nevertheless, when she went into breakfast, which was served in their suite, and found Irving alone, there was a light of battle in her dark brown eyes.

'Good,' she said with satisfaction. 'I wanted to

talk to you on your own. I think Andy and I are entitled to know why you dropped Dad and . . .'

'Rylla! Rylla!' Irving interrupted her. 'I told you last night not to jump to conclusions. I didn't drop Matt. You must accept that I don't know any more than you about his reasons. I'm as disappointed as you that he feels he can't join me. And as for Jacques, he . . .'

'Are you sure it wasn't anything to do with him?' Rylla was still only partially convinced. 'The way he pooh-poohed that article? He hasn't somehow convinced you that Dad's past it, going senile or something?'

'Of course not!' Irving's dark brows drew together in a frown. 'Would I be going on this trip, investing money in it, if I didn't trust Matt's judgement? Just as I trust he has his own good reasons for not accompanying me? I'm hurt,' he went on more quietly, 'that you could believe such things of me.'

'Oh, I'm sorry, Irving. But you must admit it's all rather odd.' Penitently she put her hand on his and, since he was not one to bear a grudge, immediately his arms engulfed her.

'Rylla, love, I wish . . .'

'*Bonjour*, Irving! M'selle Rylla!' Jacques Fresnay entered. His arrival broke through whatever Irving might have intended to say next. The Frenchman's expression was quizzical as he looked at the two of them, and some obscure instinct prompted Rylla not to move away from

Irving immediately.

She returned Jacques' greeting with a quiet 'good morning' and sat down to her breakfast. As a rule, she had a hearty appetite. But now she found herself quite unable to concentrate her attention on the food. Jacques Fresnay seemed to consider breakfast a moveable feast. He prowled about the room, talking of the forthcoming expedition, emphasising his remarks to Irving with a large hand that held either a slice of toast or a cup of coffee, as his restless meal progressed. As Rylla remembered from her student days, he was an interesting and compelling orator. But not only that. As he spoke, she found her eyes drawn to his striking appearance. This morning Jacques wore the regulation 'uniform' of the man working in warm climes: short-sleeved khaki bush shirt and trousers, so elegantly tailored to the mould of his strong body that Rylla knew immediately they had not been bought off the peg. Instinctively she recognised the unusual power and muscular beauty that his clothes only partially concealed. From time to time he glanced towards her, annoyingly catching her eyes on him.

No man, she thought with a sense of unease, had any right to such an abundance of good looks. His face was lean, the nose aquiline, his mouth wide and sensual, his cheekbones and jaw prominent. His blond hair, she considered, was badly in need of cutting. A deep tan accentuated the brilliance of his gentian-blue eyes. It was a pity Colin, her boyfriend, only just equalled Rylla's five-foot-nine. She had always preferred men she could look up to. But Jacques Fresnay was not only taller than Colin Philby, he was also far better-looking. Seen at close quarters, he was quite devastating.

She wondered if Jacques was conceited about his looks. In her experience, handsome men often were. They believed that this random gift of fate gave them the right to run riot through the hearts of susceptible women.

But she, at least, was immune, Rylla told herself. Apart from the fact that there was now Colin, she was no longer the teenager who had once succumbed to an infatuation with Jacques Fresnay, an attractive man made even more fascinating by his accent and air of foreign mystery.

CHAPTER TWO

THEY spent the whole of the next day loading the bus. Irving's urgings had moved the mechanics to greater efforts. Equipment had to be taken out of storage and reinstalled in the converted vehicle. They were carrying their own stock of basic foodstuffs, relying on villages en route for more substantial fare.

Several times during this exercise Rylla only just avoided a collision with Jacques Fresnay. To her dismay, she had soon realised that he had not lost any of his former attraction for her; and she was aware of disloyalty to Colin as once or twice she found herself speculating, just as she had done in her teens, how it would be to be held and kissed by the Frenchman. Consequently, she found herself taking exaggerated care not to brush against him in passing.

Jacques seemed to be disposed to be friendly, and addressed several bantering remarks to her, which made her laugh despite her reserve. She found herself replying in kind, to Andy's obvious disapproval.

'I don't think the aged "P" would care for you being so matey with the opposition,' he muttered once as they passed each other.

'Rubbish,' Rylla said. 'I'm only being civil to the man. Just because he disagrees with Dad doesn't make him an out-and-out villain. In fact, I rather like him. I always have,' she added unwisely.

'Of course!' Andy's eyes narrowed speculatively. 'I remember now! You used to have a crush on him, didn't you? Nearly used to freak out whenever he appeared on television.' Mockingly, 'Whatever *would* your Colin say if he knew?'

Before she could make the indignant disclaimer that Colin had no cause for worry, Irving put forward a suggestion.

'Since we're ready ahead of time, I don't think we need to wait for tomorrow morning. How about having an early dinner and travelling overnight? The traffic might be lighter.'

No one had any objection and at nine o'clock they were on the road south, the Pan American highway. It was growing dusk as the bus left Lima's rather depressing suburbs behind, and the road ran instead between cultivated fields and cacti-strewn hills.

After redesigning, only two of the original upholstered bench seats remained in the bus. These provided seating for the driver and five passengers. Irving drove, with Andy navigating. Rylla had expected that the Frenchman would also choose to sit up front, but instead he joined her on the rear seat.

With the noise of the engine, and the thrum of

the vehicle's tyres on the road surface, it was
impossible to include the pair in front in any
conversation; and Rylla felt strangely isolated
with Jacques Fresnay in a disturbing intimacy.
Despite the growing darkness of the interior, she
sensed he was watching her. He still seemed to be
in a chatty mood.

'So you are Matthew Quarmby's daughter.
Irving has spoken much of his friend's daughter.
Me, I think you do not resemble him?'

Rylla laughed. His words had conjured up an
irresistibly amusing picture.

'I should hope not! Dad has hairy caterpillar
eyebrows and a great bushy beard. I take after my
mother.'

'*Eh bien?* Then she was the beauty, your father
the brains?' As she made no reply to this impled
compliment, he went on, 'And on what subject,
M'selle Rylla, are you an authority?'

'Irving must have told you, I'm the photographer for this trip. And, though I probably
shouldn't say it myself, I *am* good at my work.' A
sudden yawn took her by surprise. 'Excuse me,
Professor Fresnay. I need some sleep. I'm tired.'

'Is it possible?' he said disbelievingly. 'Such a
big well-built girl!' If he'd been an American, he'd
have said 'well-stacked'. That was obvious from
the direction of his eyes.

'I'm not ...' she began indignantly, then
swallowed as she heard him chuckle and realised
he was being deliberately provocative. She

couldn't think why, unless it was his way of flirting with her. Perhaps Andrew was right. Perhaps she shouldn't respond too readily to his friendly overtures. 'I haven't had much rest in the past forty-eight hours,' she explained. 'So I would like to try and get some sleep, if you don't mind.' Pointedly, she leant back and closed her eyes.

'*Bien sûr*,' he said and, obligingly, 'if you would care to rest against my shoulder?'

Rylla's eyes flew open and she repressed a shiver. Alarmingly, it was not one of aversion.

'No, thank you!' Again she closed her eyes and edged further away on the deep bench seat. But her rest was fitful, since she was unable to relax totally. She was afraid she might unwittingly take advantage of his offered proximity. From time to time, she peered furtively through her thick lashes to make sure he had moved no nearer.

In the dim interior of the bus he was now just a silhouette, but she didn't need light to recall his features. In the past few hours his image seemed to have been indelibly printed on her memory cells. Even with her eyes closed, his face swam before her. Of course, she reassured herself, she *had* met him before, seen him many times on television. And in her teens she had practically worshipped him, though from afar. No wonder his features were so familiar.

It was a good twelve-hour journey down to Nasca. So it was almost ten the next morning when they branched off the Pan American highway, and entered a long stretch of bleak wilderness, the site of the famous Lines, some twenty kilometres north of Nasca itself. Here they were to pick up the last member of their expedition, Jeni Grayson, a scientist, who would be doing the Carbon-14 tests on anything they might discover.

'We're in luck!' Irving exclaimed as their party got out of the bus. 'There she is.' And Rylla saw with some awe to whom Jeni Grayson was talking. Her photographer's instinct made her stop and check her camera settings. She lined up the pair in her viewfinder. The young scientist and the unmistakable figure of the almost legendary German woman, who had spent more than four decades studying and pondering the riddle of the Nasca Lines. What a scoop for the magazine!

Introductions were made all round.

'But there is no need to introduce me to Jeni,' Jacques Fresnay protested. His wide, attractive smile was much in evidence as he took the scientist's hand in his, and she smiled up at him. 'Is that not so, *ma petite*?'

Where Rylla was tall and, some would say, statuesque, Jeni *was* petite, diminutive, all the dainty terms that applied to small, slender women. Rylla was reminded fleetingly of Gloria Ray, Colin's former girlfriend, and she wondered if Colin *was* seeing the other girl again in her absence.

Where Rylla's hair hung long, smooth and dark

about her face, Jeni's was a silver-blonde riot of curls. Her violet eyes made dull, muddy pools of Rylla's brown ones. Her piquant, gamine face made Rylla acutely conscious of her own strong bone structure and determined jaw.

They'd never met before but Rylla, while finding her own reactions to Jeni Grayson decidedly ambivalent, was in no doubt that for some reason or other the other woman didn't like her. It was not only in her voice as they were introduced, but in her speculative, assessing glances as the group chatted—Irving and Andy to the German woman, Jeni and Jacques to each other. Rylla felt suddenly excluded.

She could well believe Jacques' claim that he and Jeni were already acquainted, for they were wrangling amicably over the Nasca Lines, about which they appeared to hold opposing opinions. They seemed totally oblivious to her presence; and her sense of exclusion provoked her into a fit of most uncharacteristic pique.

'Obviously,' she directed her remark at Jeni rather than to the Frenchman, 'Professor Fresnay believes himself to be the definitive expert on the Nasca Lines, as well as on every other aspect of Peruvian history.'

'There is only one authority on the Nasca Lines.' Jacques inclined his head towards the elderly woman still in conversation with Irving. He seemed unperturbed by her oblique taunt and Rylla felt ashamed. Whatever had come over her?

She wasn't usually bitchy. '*Mais oui,*' he went on, 'I do have some small pretensions to knowledge in *other* Peruvian fields.' He had turned his long body towards her so that now she was included in a trio with him and Jeni. 'Is there, *peut-être,*' he drawled lazily, insinuatingly, 'anything further I can tell you about myself, M'selle Rylla?' His eyes ran over her in a knowledgeable assessment of her femininity. A glint in their blue depths betrayed his understanding of her chagrin.

'No, thank you,' she said quietly. She heard him chuckle as she turned and made herself stroll unconcernedly away from him. Stupid, she told herself, to let an unspoken antagonism between herself and Jeni Grayson provoke her into crossing swords with the Frenchman. She was certain she could feel his eyes boring into her back, and a sudden incomprehensible panic hastened her steps towards the bus.

Irving Wilder, together with Matthew and Andrew Quarmby, had visited the Nasca sites many times recently. This time he planned to stay only a day or two, studying the alignment of the *ceques* in the light of Matthew's new theory. With Jeni's assistance, he planned to take bearings, carbon-testing any fragments of pottery that might still be found along their length.

'Rylla, love,' Irving sounded concerned. 'You're the only one of us who hasn't been here before.' For Jeni's and Jacques' benefit he explained, 'Rylla's been to Peru once before, but only up north. Ideally she should take the opportunity to see the Nascan layout as a whole, the full scope of the designs. I'm just sorry *I* haven't got the time . . .'

'Perhaps Andy . . .?' Rylla began.

'Sorry, Sis, for that you need to be able to fly a chopper. Besides, if I can borrow a jeep I'm off down to Nasca museum, to take another look at their fantastic ceramics.'

'Perhaps M'selle Rylla would permit *me*?'

'Oh no, really, thank you,' Rylla said hastily. It might be her imagination, but it seemed to her that in the last twenty-four hours the Frenchman had gone out of his way to be attentive to her. 'If Irving hasn't got time I'm not all that bothered.' Which was ridiculous, of course, because even if professionalism did not, her heritage demanded an interest on any aspect of Peruvian antiquity. Irving's swift intervention highlighted this fact.

'Nonsense, my dear! If Jacques is kind enough to offer . . . You'll be as safe with him as with me. And Matt would never forgive me if I didn't see to it that you . . .'

'But are you and Fresnay all that concerned for Dad's feelings?' Andy put in. 'If Dad were here himself . . .'

'*Eh bien,*' Jacques put in, 'does it not occur to you that perhaps this expedition is for men younger than your father? The jungle is not . . .'

'By younger men, you mean yourself?' Andy

sneered. And, as the Frenchman gave a typically Gallic, non-committal shrug, 'And of course you haven't had much success lately, have you? You haven't been in the news for over a year, at least. So now I suppose you want to be involved in the glory of a new find. Never mind all Dad's work, his disappointment . . .'

'And you, M'selle Rylla,' Jacques looked at her. 'You agree with your brother?'

'I . . .' she began.

'Andy! Rylla!' Irving exclaimed before she could complete her sentence. 'This isn't like you, either of you. Jacques wasn't . . . he didn't . . .'

'*Non, mon ami!*' The Frenchman lifted an eyebrow. 'It is not necessary that you excuse your friends to each other. Rylla and I will fight our own battles, shall we not?' His brilliant blue eyes beneath their hooded lids were intent upon her lovely face. With her brown skin, high cheekbones and slanted eyes she could, he thought, have been a reincarnation of some long-dead Inca princess.

'I've no desire to *fight* with you, Professor Fresnay,' she began, then flushed at the misconstruction that could be—and was—put on her words.

'Nor I with you,' he said fervently, his eyes laughing at her.

Somehow, although she wasn't quite certain when or how she finally gave in, Rylla found herself in a helicopter piloted by Jacques, flying high above the famous site. For all his modest disclaimers, he did know all there was to be learned of Nascan history. He was well versed in what could only be conjecture concerning the mysterious designs and what use might have been made of them by the Incas.

'They never destroyed the cultures they conquered. In some way, they incorporated them into their own civilisation,' he told her.

Jacques was a skilful pilot and Rylla felt no fear at all as they whirled high above the desert, which was not glaring yellow sand but a very agreeable brown colour. At ground level, Jacques told her, the Lines would seem nothing more than meaningless paths. But from up here they could be seen for what they were—parts of giant triangles, beautifully drawn figures of spiders, hummingbirds, all several hundreds of feet across.

'Flying-saucer enthusiasts believed the geometric figures to be navigational aids for ancient spaceships,' Jacques informed her smilingly. 'But I prefer the more plausible theories of modern science.'

'However could they draw them when they couldn't see the finished result?' Rylla marvelled. She leant forward, absorbed, gazing down, often through the lens of her camera, until she became suddenly aware of the Frenchman's equally intent study—of her. It was more a tangible sensation than a certain knowledge. But when she turned her head abruptly, it was to find his blue eyes on her in a curiously enigmatic appraisal.

'Your face, it is a very unusual one,' he said by way of explanation. He made no apology for staring at her. Nor was she certain whether his words were intended as a compliment or criticism.

She tried to keep her voice light, cool, as though her treacherous pulses were not suddenly racing under the steady scrutiny of those sensually hooded eyes.

'I expect it's my mixed ancestry. My mother was Peruvian.'

'And your name? Rylla? That, too, is unusual. I have not heard it before.'

'It's a contraction,' she told him, 'of Amaryllis, a flower often found in Peruvian designs.'

'Amaryllis!' He rolled the 'r', repeating the name as though it were a pleasant taste on his lips. 'I like it.' Then, 'But I do *not* like that unbecoming lump in which you wear your hair at the back of your head!' His tone betrayed a more than academic interest in her thick, confined tresses. To Rylla's highly sensitised nerves, it was almost as if he had touched it.

'I don't always wear it this way. But it's convenient for my work.'

'I shall like to see it flowing loose. You are young,' he went on thoughtfully, 'to be so successful in your field?'

'Not really. I'm twenty-eight, and I probably look older.' Ruefully, 'Working in hot climates ages the skin.'

'Not so!' She hadn't been looking for compliments, but to her embarrassment he stretched out a hand, a long finger brushing the silky texture of her cheek, and she had to resist the self-conscious impulse to pass her hand over her face, erasing the sensation. 'But you are still a little young, perhaps, for Irving?' For Irving? Jacques didn't know about Colin, of course. 'He is in his fifties? You find the company of older men preferable, *peut-être*? Their maturity attractive?'

Did she? Rylla had never really thought about it. Irving was just a friend, to herself as well as to Matthew. But, some sixth sense prompted her, it might be better if Jacques believed ... especially since Colin was hundreds of miles away. She was dismayed to realise that his image was growing fainter by the minute.

'Yes,' she said slowly. 'Yes, Irving's an attractive man.' It was perfectly true. At forty-nine, Irving carried his years well. He had a pleasant countenance—what could be seen of it under the beard and moustache he'd worn as long as Rylla could remember.

'And you know him well? For a long time? He has a great fondness for you. That is evident.'

'Yes.'

'I see. And Irving is also a very wealthy man, of course.' Jacques fell into a reflective mood.

After their initial survey from the air, Jacques insisted on taking her on foot on to the pampas to demonstrate at first-hand the size and complexity of the designs.

'As you see, the desert is made up of dark brown pebbles. But just beneath the surface is a layer of yellow sand. Remove the thin top layer of pebbles, so . . .' he demonstrated, 'and you create contrasting colours.'

Even walking on the desert broke through this top layer and though, Jacques told her, in time windblown sand would fill in their footprints, the scarred surface would take centuries to heal.

'Picture to yourself, *ma chère* Rylla, in years to come the traces of our passing still to be seen. Incredible, is it not?'

It was. And it gave Rylla a strange, unfamiliar sensation to contemplate the almost-permanence of their footprints. A sensation she diagnosed incredulously as being pleasure at the sense of immortality it offered. An immortality the Frenchman would share.

'Can't say I relish the prospect of having to live off the country when we start going inland,' Andy commented next morning as they made a hearty breakfast before setting off on the next leg of their journey.

'You could always stay at base camp, *mon ami*, with the women.' Good-naturedly, Jacques teased the younger man. He did not seem to return Andrew's continued animosity. 'Irving and I will push on into the interior.'

'No way!' It was Rylla who trounced this assumption. 'I can't answer for Andy and Jeni, of course, but *I* intend to be in at the finish.'

'Oh, I'll be there, too, don't worry,' was Jeni's contribution, her violet eyes narrowing. The last two days had not seen any diminution of her veiled hostility towards Rylla. 'I wouldn't dream of letting you accompany three such attractive men unchaperoned.' To outward appearances it was a joke, so perhaps only Rylla was aware of the underlying malice.

She thought she knew the reason for the other woman's resentment—Jacques Fresnay's assiduous attentions to herself. As a friend of obviously longstanding, Jeni might well feel chagrin at the time the Frenchman was devoting to Rylla. Perhaps there had been, or still was, a closer relationship between them than mere friendship? Jeni needn't worry. It wasn't as if she, Rylla, was in competition for Jacques' favours.

'When you lot have quite finished,' Andy protested, 'I never said I wasn't going all the way. Can't a fellow even make a humorous remark without being taken up so sharply?' His glare was for the Frenchman. 'I'll be there, all the way,' he said significantly.

Aware of Irving's growing disapproval of his assistant's manner towards Jacques, Rylla changed the subject.

'I've not been into jungle terrain before. I imagine it will be very colourful? Monkeys, parrots, orchids?'

'And snakes and insects,' Jacques put in with an air of would-be innocence that didn't fool Rylla for a moment. The glint in his eyes was too revealing, as was the lifted eyebrow. Like a fool, during general conversation, she'd admitted her aversion to snakes.

'Oh, I don't suppose snakes and insects will be the only pests around,' she said ambiguously and saw the blue eyes spark momentarily. Damn! It wasn't like her to be provocative towards men, and she had the oddest feeling that Jacques had stored her remark up for retaliation.

As to the wildlife, Rylla comforted herself, she would be protected by her trousers, tucked into high leather boots. There were mosquito nets to discourage winged creatures by night, and spray repellents for daytime use. They would be carrying guns, but she hoped they would meet nothing requiring such a drastic deterrent. No, it wasn't anything native to the jungle she feared. The only threat to her peace of mind was much closer to hand and infinitely more dangerous. But she was still confident in the talisman of her love for Colin and her own ability to cope with the situation.

When later they left Nasca, Irving driving once more, Rylla closed her eyes. Concern for her father's disappointment, his directive concerning the Frenchman, her own complicated reactions to Jacques Fresnay, meant she hadn't been sleeping too well. Soon she was dozing, inhabiting a no-man's land of half-waking dreams, in which Jacques and an enormous boa constrictor pursued her with equally deadly menace.

Apart from necessary stops, including those to swop drivers, they pressed on, once again driving through the night. At one of their stops just after dawn, Irving relinquished the wheel to Jacques. Irving insisted that Rylla and Andy occupy the front bench, so they might have a better view as they entered Arequipa, a town of quaint old Spanish houses and hefty churches. Arequipa, standing at the gateway between the coast and the sierra, had perhaps the most beautiful situation in Peru, overlooked by a trio of volcanoes, their snow-capped peaks still lost in a haze of morning mist as the bus wound into the valley.

Rylla had hoped to avoid sitting next to Jacques. The sheer sexual chemistry he exuded, without any apparent effort on his part, still troubled her. But Andy had politely ushered her ahead of him, and however hard she tried, it was impossible to avoid physical contact with the Frenchman. A strange tingling warmth assailed her flesh whenever his arm accidentally brushed against hers, whenever her thigh was confined against the hard muscularity of his.

For a moment, an unexpectedly sensual sensation swamped her and she swallowed. She closed her eyes for an instant against the scenery—the road running between two lakes, through green pastures dotted with dry peaks to fertile pampas. This was insanity, she couldn't be feeling this way! She shivered convulsively and made greater efforts to edge away from him on the seat that was only just wide enough to accommodate three people. He angled her a sideways glance.

'Cold? Surely not?'

He knew darned well she couldn't be cold. Though it was early, the temperature was already soaring inside the bus. She was sure he knew what had made her shiver, and the certainty unsettled her. But if she were to make a further move, or insist on changing seats again so soon, it would confirm his knowledge of the effect he had on her. She gritted her teeth and tried to concentrate on sensations of another kind—hunger, thirst, the need for sleep in a comfortable bed instead of a sleeping-bag on the hard ground.

Irving had agreed they should find overnight accommodation in Arequipa. They could freshen up and do vital laundry, and Irving planned to spend some time in the University museum, now the repository of de Molina's original manuscript.

'Besides, I've given the museum as a poste-restante address for any mail,' he told them. 'There won't be much communication with the outside world shortly.'

Finding a place to stay proved to be no problem. The *pension* to which they were directed was set around a pretty colonial-style courtyard, shaded by eucalyptus trees. Their long dark branches hung like screens behind the buildings. A fountain played lazily in the centre of the tiled yard. Andy disappeared almost immediately after they had eaten, and Irving announced his intention of going directly to the museum in the hope of finding the archivist, Pedro Garcia, free.

'Want to come along, Jeni?' he asked the scientist, and Rylla knew a spurt of resentment that he hadn't included her in his invitation. On her previous trip she'd gone everywhere with him and Matthew.

Her feelings must have shown in her face, for, '*Eh bien?*' Jacques said. 'It seems we are left, once again, to occupy ourselves. You have a preference?'

'Yes,' Rylla said hastily. 'I want to go to bed.' And then, as his eyebrow quirked aloft, furious with herself for her careless tongue, 'I—I mean, I'm tired. It's been a long journey, without proper rest.'

'*Naturellement!* What else?' he agreed with a bland courtesy that did not for one moment deceive her. Oh, he was a master of *double entendre*, conveyed by just the faintest lift of that annoying eyebrow, or a slight lowering of those heavy lids. 'But when you are rested, *peut-être?*'

'Then,' she said, evenly polite, 'I'd rather explore on my own, thank you. I'm a photographer and other people find it very boring.'

She did lie down on her bed. But though she could have sworn she would sleep, an hour later she was still wide awake and speculating, not on the possibility of their mission's success as she ought to be, but on Jacques Fresnay. His professional exploits were well known, but the man behind the public figure had always remained an enigma. She wondered what he was like when he was with his intimates, with those he loved. Come on, she told herself, don't pussyfoot around the subject. What you want to know is if there's a woman in his life.

Restlessly Rylla shook her head from side to side, as though the physical movement could eject such thoughts. It was no use, sleep could not be wooed. The room was hot and stuffy despite the ceaselessly whirring fans. She might just as well get up and go out. Once he'd contacted Garcia and seen the antique manuscript for himself, Irving wouldn't want to loiter in Arequipa. He would want to push on. She ought to take this opportunity to look around.

She freshened up, changing her shabby jeans and shirt for a brightly coloured cotton skirt and blouse. Hung around with cameras and light meters, she stepped out on to the central courtyard. When she saw the tall figure lounging indolently against the fountain she turned instantly on her heel, intending to beat a speedy retreat. Too late; she had been observed. Jacques straightened and strolled towards her. The brilliant sunshine made a dazzling halo of his almost lint-white hair.

'You are feeling rested now? *Bon!* Shall we go?'

'I did say I'd rather look round on my own,' she reminded him.

'But you do not know Arequipa, Rylla, *ma chère*. And your time here is limited. Accompanied by one who knows, you will see far more of what is important. So come.'

He tucked a hand beneath her unwilling elbow, in a gesture incredibly difficult to reject without seeming to make too much of it. And so she suffered his touch as he ushered her into the *collectivo* he had hailed to take them to their first objective. But she was unable to prevent a slight flinching, a stiffening of her body which did not pass unobserved.

'*Eh bien?*' he said, looking enquiringly at her. Because of the vehicle's other occupants she was unable to sit as far away from him as she would have wished. 'You seem uneasy? You are nervous of me for some reason. I think?'

Once let him think *that*, guess the reason for it, and she was lost. A man of his sort might well see her determined reserve as a challenge.

'I'm not at all nervous,' she told him mendaciously. 'I just prefer not to be manhandled by strangers. And I hate being jostled.' She indicated their fellow passengers.

'Ah! I see!' The trouble was, she felt he had seen through the excuse. 'As for the journey,' he shrugged, 'it will not be a long one. As to you and me . . . After a while we shall not be strangers. We shall be many weeks together, is it not so? And no reason then why we should not be friends. I think, *ma chère* Rylla, that at the moment you are *not* friendly towards me? Because I have replaced your father on this expedition?'

She avoided a direct answer about her feelings towards him. 'Considering your views on the subject, I'm surprised you wanted to come on this trip.'

'*Comment?*'

'Well, isn't it rather a waste of your time and money to go on what you obviously consider to be a wild-goose chase?'

'Wild goose? Ah, you mean the fruitless expedition? But what makes you think these are my views?'

'You made them crystal-clear in that letter you wrote last year, about my father's article on Atahualpa.'

'Ah, it is so?' He quirked an eyebrow at her. 'Of course! I see. I had forgotten.'

'You'd *forgotten?*' she said incredulously.

'I regret——' He didn't sound in the least regretful, but irritatingly cheerful. 'I write many things. I do not always recall the names of those whom I . . .'

'Criticise and ridicule,' she suggested drily.

He did not reply immediately. There was much Rylla would have liked to see in the beautiful eighteenth-century city. Not least, the colonial churches with their elaborately carved façades of *sillar*, a soft white stone composed of volcanic ash. But their taxi had pulled up outside a museum and Jacques was engaged in paying off the driver. He ushered Rylla in through the doors, a courtesy that once more set her unsettled nerves on edge.

'Ridicule?' he said at last, as he steered her towards a display of pottery and stonework from the Chavin civilisation. '*Mais non!* Naturally I criticise where it is necessary. But ridicule? *Non.* It is not polite to ridicule those less informed than oneself.'

'Less informed?' Rylla said incredulously. Her voice rose an octave, careless of the attendant's interested gaze. 'Haven't you forgotten something, Professor Fresnay?' With a proud tilt of her dark head, she emphasised, 'All my father's years of knowledge and experience?'

'I did not of course, include your father among the less informed. But this, I must say. Age and experience themselves do not always guarantee certain knowledge, or freedom from error. You see, Rylla, *ma chère* . . .'

'I wish you'd stop calling me that. And I don't remember giving you permission to use my first name, either. I . . .' Her voice trailed away. She saw his eyebrow rise, its lift of puzzled enquiry making her feel foolish.

'It is that I must apply for permission?' There was unflagging good humour in his voice. Rylla wished he wasn't so good-natured, so eminently likeable. It would be much easier to preserve her immunity to his attractions. 'But we were introduced by our first names, *n'est-ce pas*? And I am most agreeable that you should call me by mine. On a trip such as we undertake, formality is out of place, *non*? But we digress. Your father's paper, though well written, was in error in that . . .'

'But he researches his work thoroughly. He . . .'

'*Peut-être!*' Jacques said, one large, beautiful hand raised pacifyingly. 'The mistake lies not in his research. It is in his presentation as certainty what can only be theory.'

'Theory! When we *know* Atahualpa's descendants went into hiding after the Spaniards killed him? When we know that the Spanish didn't find all the Inca gold?'

'*Vraiment!* But gently, *ma chère*. This we know, I agree.' His enthusiasm matched hers. He leant forward across the glass case that divided them, and laid a hand on hers. 'But we must not forget. At the time of Atahualpa, the Inca empire was divided. There was already civil war before the Spanish invasion.'

'But you can't honestly believe——' carefully she withdrew her hand '—that a man like my father isn't aware of such basic facts? Everyone knows Pizarro took advantage of the conflict between the son of the Inca's mistress and his lawful son, Huascar.'

But Jacques had moved around the showcase to stand at her side.

'Before Atahualpa had his half-brother assassinated, who is to say which brother despatched gold to the Sacred City, or where that city lies? If the lost city is in Northern Peru close to Quito, yes, maybe Atahualpa himself was responsible. But suppose, *ma chère*, as your father seems to, that the lost city lies in Southern Peru? Is it not then more reasonable to suppose that it was Huascar, the rightful heir who ruled from Cuzco, who concealed the gold? Not from the Spaniards, but at an earlier time, from his rapacious and treacherous brother?'

'And yet . . .' But she was not allowed to speak. Jacques' earnest blue eyes held hers, as did the touch of his hand on her shoulder.

'Remember, too, Atahualpa had promised the Spaniard much gold in exchange for his own wretched life. Did he intend that Huascar's wealth be included in that ransom? If you had been Huascar, would you have been willing to see your rightful inheritance form part of such a transaction?'

'No, I suppose not,' Rylla said slowly. Jacques sounded so certain, to one who had always been accustomed to accepting her father's word as law. 'But,' triumphantly, 'as you pointed out, *all* of this is conjecture, including yours. Why should your theory be any more certain than my father's?'

'No reason at all, *ma chère* Rylla.' Uneasily, she wished he wouldn't persist in calling her that, her name dropping silkenly from his tongue. The rolled 'R' and his accent gave it a caressing sound.

But it wasn't an endearment, she reminded herself, any more than were the 'darlings' readily exchanged in certain strata of society. 'But I am more ready, apparently, than you or your father, to admit this. So,' he grinned at her, the hand on her shoulder moving caressingly, 'shall we agree upon a truce? And wait to see which one of us, if either, is proved correct? Could we not also be . . . friends?'

She was silent. Common sense told her he could be right about one thing. Her much-loved father, from whom she inherited her own impulsive enthusiasms, might have been a little too precipitate, too dogmatic in his presentation of his findings; though he would never admit as much. Yet Ryłła was unwilling to concede any victory to this man. She had an uneasy feeling that in the lesser conquest might lie the risk of a greater, more dangerous one.

'Rylla?' She realised he was still waiting for her answer.

'As to Atahualpa,' she said slowly, 'I suppose we can only agree to differ until we find out. But you can't expect me to feel very friendly towards you. Not when you've taken my father's place.

The handsome face did not harden with displeasure as she'd expected, but broke up into a smile so attractive that it riveted her gaze upon him, her eyes widening in involuntary awareness of its compulsion. Her heart bumped rapidly. For a moment, she'd thought he was about to kiss her.

And equally, for a briefer instant, she'd wanted him to.

'Believe me, Rylla, *ma chère*,' he said with heavy emphasis, 'your father's place is the last place in your life I would wish to fill.'

She wasn't naïve enough to ask him what he meant. That was crystal-clear. She was relieved not to have to answer his remark by anything other than a quelling flash of her dark eyes. For, as they left the display of Chavin artefacts, they encountered Irving and Jeni.

'Irving, how nice!' Rylla greeted the other man with a palpable pleasure, born of relief. Though Jeni, she suspected, was less than enchanted by their meeting. 'I didn't know you were coming here. Is this where . . .?'

'No, no. But we've seen Molina's manuscript. Incredible!' Irving enthused. 'To think it should have survived and yet lain undiscovered all these years. We had time to spare, so we thought we'd take a look at the exhibits here. This is more your scene, isn't it, Jacques?'

'*Mais oui!* My real love is for the pre-Inca civilisations.' The Frenchman's blue eyes were alight now with almost obsessive enthusiasm. This was how she preferred him, Rylla thought, the professional man rather than the flirtatious dilettante. His grasp of the subject was phenomenal. And at least she could admire his brain, his scholarship, without feeling any disloyalty towards Colin Philby. 'The Chavin,' Jacques was saying, 'were the earliest pottery culture of the north-east coast. Of all the products of the human hand and brain, for me pottery, with its painted, modelled or incised decoration, comes nearest to writing. Especially since, *hélas*, in Peru there are no written records.'

The four of them completed their sightseeing as a group. Rylla was pleased, though she guessed Jeni wasn't. Irving took over the leadership, his hand often on Rylla's arm, as he made sure she did not miss items of particular architectural beauty.

'So the manuscript *was* genuine?' she asked him. 'Dad was right?' Out of the corner of her eye she noted that once again Jacques and Jeni seemed to be getting on famously.

'Undoubtedly genuine,' Irving confirmed. 'But, Rylla, you know I have tremendous faith in Matt's theories. Sometimes they're based on what seems almost like intuition. But he's rarely mistaken. Surely *you* never doubted . . .?'

'Of course not. But Professor Fresnay doesn't share your faith in Dad, does he?'

'Rylla, my dear!' Irving's manner was gentle as he placed an arm about her shoulders. But beneath his words she sensed rebuke. 'If our mission is to stand any chance of success, we must all work together in harmony.'

'*C'est vrai!*' the Frenchman put in before Rylla could answer. 'And I assure you, *mon ami*, this aversion Rylla has for me—of a surety, it is one-sided.' His blue eyes rested boldly on her face. '*I* am most willing to admire.'

'It isn't aversion . . .' she began hotly, then blushed, relieved when Irving interrupted her impulsive denial.

'But then, Rylla and Andy have been labouring under a misapprehension,' Irving said, 'which until now I've been powerless to dispel, purely due to lack of information. Perhaps now she'll believe me when I tell her I was as puzzled as anyone by Matt's extraordinary defection. And that you and I were *not* involved in any conspiracy to exclude him from this expedition.' He turned to Rylla. 'There was a letter for me from Matt, with an enclosure for you. I'd intended to wait until we were alone. But now I think you'd better read his letter to me aloud.'

Unsuspectingly, Rylla took the proffered missive. She thrust her own letter into the side pocket of her camera case, then ran her eyes over the familiar writing. A stifled gasp escaped her and she read on more carefully, agonising over every word. At last she looked up at Irving speechlessly, her eyes full of tears. She swallowed.

'He's been ill—*is* ill,' she said.

'Aloud, Rylla,' Irving said, gently but inexorably.

'Dear Irving,' Matthew Quarmby had written, 'you must be wondering why an old trouper such as I let you down at the eleventh hour and why, as your friend, I gave you no explanation. The truth is, I was afraid you wouldn't be able to keep it from that shrewd, impulsive daughter of mine. And I didn't want Rylla and Andy to come galloping home unnecessarily. Not until I'd had the results of certain tests, anyway. As it turns out, it's nothing too serious, only angina. With care, I could still make it to a hundred.' Matthew was sixty-five. 'But I think you'll agree, the high altitudes of Peru, plus traipsing through jungle, wouldn't be exactly beneficial to the old codger I must now admit I've become. Forgive me, old friend? The enclosed is for Rylla. Don't let her be too angry with me, either. And take care of her for me.'

'Irving!' Rylla said urgently. 'Do you think he's telling the truth—that he's not too ill?' She had quite forgotten their silent companions, and her tears spilled over. 'I couldn't bear to lose him. He's been everything to me and Andy since our mother ... And, oh, Irving, I *am* sorry I misjudged you. I ...' She couldn't go on.

Irving pulled her against his broad chest.

'I don't think he'd lie about a thing like that,' he said comfortingly. 'Not worrying you until necessary is one thing. But if it had been really serious he would have wanted you home, surely?'

'You don't think I ought to go home, anyway?' Rylla said. All her instincts were to do so.

'No, I'm sure that would be the last thing he'd want. He'd want you to go ahead and be in on this discovery, on his behalf.'

'Well, I shall telephone him, anyway.' Rylla

looked about her vaguely, as if expecting a telephone kiosk to materialise.

'Of course. I would have suggested it myself. We'll book the call as soon as we get back to the *pension*. But first,' gently, but insistently, 'don't you think you owe someone else an apology?'

She bit her lip and slanted a sideways glance to where Jacques stood. During her moment of distress Jeni had politely averted her eyes. But the Frenchman was still watching her, his expression speculative as he looked from her to Irving and back again. She wasn't reluctant to apologise, only apprehensive as to how it would be received.

'Jacques left home and another important task at only a few hours' notice, so that I did not have to cancel my arrangements.' Having said which, Irving walked on ahead with Jeni, leaving Rylla to confront the Frenchman alone.

'I would suggest,' Jacques said, 'that we go directly to the *telefonos*. That is usually the most productive place to try when putting through an international call.'

'Jacques, I . . .' She didn't notice she'd used his name for the first time.

'It is impossible, unfortunately, to estimate how long this will take—three minutes or three hours.'

'Jacques, please! Please let me apologise to you.'

'Your apology is already accepted, *ma chère* Rylla.'

'But you haven't let me apologise properly.'

'What had you in mind?' Never had that dark

eyebrow elevated itself so perilously. 'Do you wish, as *les enfants* say, to kiss and make up?'

'Oh, no! I ...'

'For, if so,' the blue eyes were lit with mischief, 'I should prefer to choose the time and the place. Somewhere less public.'

'Oh, you're impossible!' Rylla exploded, but it was a very feeble eruption and she let him lead her towards the telephone exchange. After only half an hour's nail-biting delay, she was connected with her father.

'Oh, Dad!' was all she could say at first, in choked, tearful tones. His voice brought him so clearly to mind. Then though she already knew the answer, 'Why didn't you tell me before?'

Only when both Matthew and then her aunt had assured her that his condition was not serious, but easily controlled by rest and tablets, would she consent to relinquish the instrument. And it was only when she saw Jacques produce a bankers' card that she realised the price of her reassurance. But it was worth it.

'I'll pay you back as soon as I can,' she told him gratefully as they emerged into the street. It was difficult to maintain her reserve with someone who had been witness to her deepest emotions, someone who had been of such practical assistance. 'You must tell me what I owe you.' As she looked up at him, her face had still not lost all its vulnerable softness, and Jacques drew in a long breath.

'Only this.' With a neat, deft movement that took her totally by surprise, he drew her into a shadowy crevice between two buildings and she was immobilized beneath his kiss. It was only a short one, but it had a shattering effect, making her breathless and confused so that unthinkingly she found herself returning it. Only when Jacques freed her and stared down into her bemused brown eyes, his own enigmatic, when she heard his murmured *'Eh bien!* Is it possible?' did Rylla realise exactly what had happened.

'Is what possible?' she asked suspiciously, but Jacques was not to be drawn. Instead, he took possession of her hand. He tucked it firmly through his arm and suggested they return to the *pension* and reassure Irving and Andy as to Matthew's condition.

As she matched his brisk pace, Rylla's brain ticked over as fast and as furiously as the click of her sandalled heels on the roadway. There was something she had to say to Jacques, and she found herself at a loss for the words to say it.

'You are very silent, *ma chère* Rylla,' he quizzed her after a while. 'Is it that you are still unhappy about *le bon père*?'

'No,' she said slowly. 'That is, I suppose I'll still be a bit anxious until I get home and see for myself he's all right. It's . . .' Get it over with, she adjured herself. 'It's just that I don't want you to—to get any ideas.'

'Comment?' he said unhelpfully, as she hesitated.

'I don't want you to think,' she rushed on, unable to choose her words with the care she would have wished, 'that kiss meant . . .'

'*Oui?*'

'Meant you can take liberties. I'm very grateful. You've been very kind, but I don't . . .'

'Go in for casual relationships?' he suggested with a sudden suspicious mastery of English.

'Yes,' she said with relief. 'I'm here as a member of the team. But I . . .'

'But not to provide a little light relief for its male members?' Again his command of colloquial expressions belied his earlier apparent incomprehension.

'I'm glad you understand.'

'*Non!*' He shook his head, smiled wryly. '*Moi, je comprends rien.* But I hope to become better informed very soon. And we are no longer enemies? That is so?'

'We were never enemies,' she protested. 'But it's only fair to tell you, Professor Fresnay, I'll do all I can towards proving my father's theory.'

'At least continue to call me Jacques,' he murmured persuasively. 'You say it so prettily, *ma chère* Rylla'

'Very well, Jacques,' she conceded, concerned to find herself blushing. 'Just as long as you remember . . .'

'That a kiss means nothing? But of course!' His eyebrows lifted. 'Nothing at all!'

CHAPTER THREE

JACQUES' ready agreement with her ought to have been reassuring. But somehow it wasn't. During their evening meal, Rylla watched him talking animatedly to Jeni. She found herself wondering how many women had been misled by that caressing warmth in his voice as he said their names. How many had seen his kisses as a token of something more profound? Yet he'd said a kiss meant nothing.

To divert her mind from the more and more intriguing subject of Jacques Fresnay, she began to quiz Irving about the expedition.

'Where do we stop next?' she asked him.

'Pedro Garcia has recommended a guide experienced in jungle survival. He's accompanied other groups in the past, and been found reliable and trustworthy.'

'Where do we find this paragon?' Andy asked. He was engaged in—as he put it—'stocking his internal larder since you never know on these trips where the next square meal is coming from.'

'We'll pick him up at Puno.' And, for Rylla's benefit, 'That's about twelve hours from here, on the edge of Lake Titicaca. Angel, as Garcia calls him—apparently his second name is unpronounceable—is an Aymara Indian. The Aymara farm the land around Titicaca.'

'And this Angel would be willing to leave his farm for all that length of time to guide us?' Rylla asked doubtfully.

'Oh, yes. He's the youngest son of six, dispensable for a month or two.'

'So when do we leave?' Andy enquired between mouthfuls.

'Why not now, after this meal? Since Rylla's made her phone call, there's nothing to keep us. And it's worked well so far, travelling overnight.'

'Gee whizz, Irving!' Andy complained. 'I thought we were staying here for at least one night. I was really looking forward to that bed.'

'Not to mention another *pension* breakfast?' Jacques enquired, fascinated blue eyes observing Andy's non-stop intake of food. But his pleasantry was ignored. Andy was carrying his animosity a bit too far, Rylla thought. She resolved to speak to him the first chance she got.

'I'll put it to the vote,' Irving suggested. 'Those in favour of moving on?' And, since Andy was the only dissenter, 'Right, I'll drive the first leg. Jeni, you sit up front with me. Andy, you can navigate.'

Which meant, Rylla thought with a nervous convulsion of her throat, she would have to share the remaining seat with Jacques.

'I don't mind navigating for you, Irving,' she offered a little breathlessly. 'Andy sounds ready for sleep. But I'm wide awake.'

'Thanks, love, but Andy and I know this road. We've travelled it before. You haven't.'

'Good try, *ma chère!*' Jacques murmured throatily under cover of the general conversation. 'But it would seem fate is determined to throw us together.'

'I don't believe in fate,' she retorted smartly. 'I believe in directing my own destiny.'

It was ridiculous to be so edgy, Rylla told herself firmly, as she replaced the few items she had removed from her suitcase. It wasn't as if she were going to be alone with the Frenchman. With three other people on the bus he could hardly ... Other men had flirted with her. It had been enjoyable. She had parried their attentions lightly. But the thought of her inevitable proximity to Jacques Fresnay for the first part of the journey, at least, reduced her to a quivering tension.

She slammed the suitcase shut and hurried out to the bus. The others were already aboard, waiting for her. Irving, who was obviously impatient to be on his way, had the engine running. As Rylla edged behind the front seat to reach her place, the bus moved forward, throwing her off balance, precipitating her into the last place she wanted to be—Jacques Fresnay's arms. She lay spreadeagled across his knees, her face pressed to a broad chest beneath which a strong heart thudded a beat that her own pulses took up and accelerated.

'*Eh bien!*' he breathed in her ear. His arm

tightened about her and she felt laughter shake his chest. 'Who said we would not be thrown together? When you effect a reconciliation, you do so with enthusiasm.'

'It was an accident, as you very well know,' she hissed, trying vainly to extricate herself. And, more urgently, 'Let go of me!' For, in breaking her fall, one of his large, shapely hands had curved around her hip and still restrained her. More alarmingly, the other had fleetingly brushed against her breast, and to her mortification she knew her nipples had hardened in response to his touch.

With a solicitude that further unnerved her, he helped her into her half of the bench seat, where she promptly sat as far away from him as possible. She felt his mocking sideways appraisal and heard him chuckle as she so determinedly distanced herself from him.

Soon the blanketing darkness beyond the vehicle's windows, the thrum of its tyres, the hum of conversation from the front seat, had their soporific effect upon Rylla. Heavy-eyed, she found herself regretting the afternoon's missed opportunity to catch up on her sleep. Several times her head jolted uncomfortably and she caught herself back from the edge of slumber. Finally, not even her hardy determination could keep her eyes open.

It was wonderful, this comfort, this feeling of security. Her head was pillowed against something reassuringly supportive. The darkness around her was an intimate cocoon, enclosing her in warm awareness of well-being. Rylla was unable to see beyond vague silhouetted shapes, and her blindness heightened her other senses. She heard the steady, rhythmic pulse of something close beneath her ear. Her nostils attuned themselves to a sharp, sweet scent of—masculine cologne?

Her pleasant lethargy was dispelled by dismayed realisation. While she'd slept, Jacques had edged closer to her. It was against his chest that her head rested. His arm encircled her firmly even when, fully conscious, she tried to jerk away.

'And you claimed to be so wide awake!' he mocked gently. Then, 'Relax, *mon enfant! Restes tranquille!*' His strongly accented voice murmured the soothing words against her hair. 'You will need all your strength in the days ahead, if the going is not to prove too hard for you.'

'I'm quite capable of keeping up with the rest of you.' Rylla increased her efforts to free herself, efforts which seemed remarkably ineffective. 'And I'm not your child!' She was suddenly aware that she preferred his previously drawled *'ma chère'*, aware of her body's pleasurable reaction to the closeness of his.

'*C'est vrai.* You are not a child. With that, I am in complete agreement!' There was a certain huskiness underlying the amusement in his voice. Rylla knew with an irritating certainty that if she could see his face the laughter would show there, too, and that her attempts to break free of his arms were only emphasising her soft femininity. 'You are a very lovely young woman.' Throatily, he confirmed what she already feared, his awareness of her. 'But so cold, so remote. *Pourquoi?*'

'Better than being an easy target!' she retorted, making light of his accusation.

'*Comment?*'

Again she tried to prise loose the hands clamped so firmly about her waist.

'I mean that I told you not to get any ideas. I hope you didn't think I was the sort to succumb to the first pass you . . .?'

'Not the *first?*' he enquired interestedly. He was still laughing at her.

'Not the second, *not any!*' she told him. The engine noise made it necessary to speak loudly, and she was afraid their conversation would be overheard.

'What *would* it take, *ma chère* Rylla?' It was a threatening growl, his voice expressing his certainty that *he* possessed whatever was necessary.

Valiantly she fought against his insistent hand, now transferred from her waistline to her chin, which was inexorably turning her face up to his.

'Why are you *doing* this?' was the final desperate whisper that escaped her lips, before his dipped to claim them. 'When I've told you . . .'

'Because, *peut-être*,' he said between soft, short, unsatisfying kisses, 'I do not believe you. Because, *peut-être*, I think you protest too much.' The short kisses became longer, more intense.

Somehow she had expected his kiss would be an assertive attempt to dominate. Instead, it was incredibly gentle. His mouth coaxed, persuaded hers, until the heat rushed up inside her. Her lips softened so that at last they moulded to his. The sudden upsurge of physical desire was frightening in its intensity, a total contradiction of her own beliefs. This wasn't fair to Colin. Panic galvanised her into renewed resistance.

This time, as she wrenched away from him, he made no attempt to prevent her, but his chuckle held an infuriating note of satisfaction. The wave of desire his kiss had aroused was swamped, chilled to anger, not just at him but at her own weakness.

'Irving!' She reached forward and touched the driver's shoulder. She took a deep breath to smooth the ragged note from her voice. 'Could I sit up front for a bit? I get sick travelling in the back.'

'Little liar!' Jacques murmured tenderly, but she ignored him.

'No problem,' Irving said. 'Jeni, change places with Rylla, will you?' And, as he braked, 'Want to get out for a breath of air?'

'No, thanks. I don't want to hold you up. I'll be all right if I can just sit up here with you.'

But it was some while before her shaken nerves settled. She was still angry, but as much with herself as with the Frenchman. She should have been quite capable of handling the situation with cool aplomb. But he'd caught her off guard, she excused herself. Her fatigue had betrayed her. Also, physically, he was so much stronger.

But overriding all Rylla's indignation was the shameful knowledge that for a moment he had won a response from her. He was too experienced a man not to have recognised it. And it was going to be difficult to forget the taste of his kiss, the firm muscularity of his body against hers, that frenzied stir of physical longing that Colin had never aroused in her.

She didn't want this added complication to the expedition. Bad enough that, for Matthew's sake, she must challenge the Frenchman in his professional field, without having the strain of resisting his effect upon her. But at last the fatigue she had been fighting for days overcame her once more. Her last coherent thought as her head dropped sideways was that it was safe to sleep against Irving's shoulder.

'Wakey-wakey, sleepy head!' The deep rumble of Irving's voice beneath her ear stirred her, and she realised it was daylight, that the bus had stopped.

'Where are we?' Rylla raised her head and ran her hands through the dark tangle of hair which had become unfastened from the nape of her neck. She looked about her.

'Puno.'

'Heavens! I must have slept for hours.'

'So much so,' Jeni put in tartly, 'that Irving

hasn't had a break. He refused to disturb you to change drivers.'

'I'm sorry, Irving,' Rylla said contritely as she eased her cramped limbs from the now stationary bus.

'No need to apologise, love.' The big man gave her one of his affectionate hugs. 'You can sleep against my shoulder any time. You mustn't let us forget that you're not a tough old hand like the rest of us.'

'And if you can't stand the pace,' Jeni put in with what *sounded* like sweet reason, but Rylla sensed was not, 'it would be better to admit it before the going gets even tougher. An expedition is only as good as its weakest member.'

'Thanks for the advice.' Rylla smiled with bright insincerity. 'But I think you'll find I'm no weakling. My work makes tough physical demands on me.' She tucked a hand through Irving's arm, the other through Andy's. Let Jeni keep Jacques amused, she thought.

Yet she couldn't prevent herself from listening to their companionable conversation, as their little party wended its way through the cobbled streets of Puno to the market-place. Here, Irving had been told, he would almost certainly find Angel, the Aymara Indian who was to be their guide.

'What do you think you're playing at?' Andy asked his sister at the first opportunity, when no one else was within hearing. And, as she looked at him uncomprehendingly, 'Nobody else noticed what was going on in the back seat. But I did.'

'Nothing was going on.'

'Not much! I know you've always fancied Fresnay, but to encourage him like that, a man who's ousted Dad ...'

'I wasn't encouraging him,' she said fiercely. 'He just ...'

'Made a pass at you, did he?' Andy scowled. 'Cheeky bastard! If he wasn't bigger than me I'd ...'

'I'm quite capable of dealing with Professor Fresnay,' Rylla said hurriedly. There was enough bad feeling between her brother and the Frenchman as it was.

'If you say so! I'd have said something there and then and broken it up, but I didn't want Irving to know what was going on.'

'It has nothing to do with Irving. Look, Andy, for the last time, I am not interested in Irving in that way. If you want to take exception on anyone's behalf it should be Colin's. Now, let's drop the subject, shall we?'

'OK. OK. But just remember who Fresnay is and what he's done.'

'I haven't forgotten. But I think you're going overboard a bit in the way you treat him. Just take it easy, hmm?'

Her brother fell into a sullen silence, broken after a while by a sudden thought.

'Irving said Dad enclosed a personal note for us. What did it say?'

'Goodness!' Rylla clapped a hand to her mouth. 'I didn't open it. In the rush to try and phone home, I . . . Where on earth did I put it? It must be still in my skirt pocket, in my case. Remind me to look for it later, will you?'

As Andy and Irving made enquiries of the stall holders, Rylla studied their wares. There were prune-sized purple potatoes, bananas, avocados, edible seaweeds. She paused occasionally to inspect a painted clay bowl, a glazed figure or quaintly formed talisman. The stallholders were mainly women. Their colourful, umbrella-like skirts contrasted strangely with the ugly felt derbies worn atop their coiled black braids. There were a few men dressed in ill-fitting, dusty black suits of European design. Their wares were more exotic—iguanas, tortoises, parrots, cockatoos.

'*Eh bien!* Watch out for their beaks! They can give you a nasty nip.'

Rylla jerked back the exploratory hand she had extended, and swung around sharply. But she was less afraid of the bird than of finding herself separated from Irving. It was the Frenchman who stood at her side.

'Irving sent me back to look for you,' Jacques explained blandly. 'He's found not Angel, but his wife. They come here regularly to sell the produce from the family farm. But,' with a wry smile for the vagaries of his sex, 'Angel leaves the commercial side to his wife.'

Unwillingly, Rylla fell into step at his side,

tensely conscious of his guiding hand that hovered but did not quite touch her elbow. Unable to prevent the involuntary reaction, she shuddered. Touching her or not, the chemistry still prevailed.

'*Qu'est-ce que tu as?*' Jacques asked solicitously.

'I'm a bit cold.' Swiftly she excused her tremor and added, 'I left my extra sweater on the bus.'

Jacques put his arm about her shoulders.

'Is that any better? Here we are at a greater altitude. The month of May is the beginning of winter. But that will make very little difference when we go into the jungle.' She was conscious of him looking down at her from his greater height, one eyebrow queryingly aloft. As they walked, thigh brushed against thigh. 'You do realise it is going to be uncomfortably hot and humid, *ma chère*? And that it may be dangerous? In places, we may have to cut our way through. We shall be on foot, sleeping in tents and——' was that a hint of laughter in his voice? '—looking out for snakes!'

'All right!' She halted. Glad of any excuse to draw away from him, she pretended more indignation than she felt. She faced him hands on hips. She met the vivid blue eyes squarely. 'So you know I don't like snakes! But I'm not a coward, Jacques. I'll get acclimatised to the weather, and I'm going to be there when Irving finds Atahualpa's gold.' She ignored his contradictory, 'Huascar's gold.'

'You are very loyal to your father, you and your

brother,' he said as they moved on, forcing their way through the noisy, milling crowd. She was relieved that he'd made no attempt to place his arm about her again. 'It is a most admirable quality. Though I could wish Andrew were a little less belligerent in his championship. I have never met Matthew Quarmby in the flesh. What kind of man is he, I wonder, to inspire such devotion?' It was said musingly, as if to himself, but Rylla felt impelled to give an emphatic answer.

'One of the most brilliant men alive.' Challengingly, 'The foremost expert in his field.' Sparkling dark eyes dared him to deny it.

'And he is all the family you and your brother have?'

'We have an aunt,' Rylla told him, and he watched closely as her voice and eyes softened.

'You are fond of her, *non*?'

'Very,' she said simply.

When Rylla's mother had died fifteen years ago, Ida Quarmby, only forty-five and at the height of her own career, had unselfishly given up her teaching position and gone to live in the rambling old Tudor house in Chester. She had insisted on acting as housekeeper to her somewhat eccentric older brother, and as surrogate mother to her thirteen-year-old niece and nine-year-old nephew. It couldn't have been easy at first, Rylla knew, coping with a bereaved man who had guarded his wounds like a baffled, ill-tempered lion, and two equally unhappy children. At first,

Rylla had bitterly resented her aunt. But gradually her affectionate nature had been won over by Ida's transparent goodness. Childhood love was now a firm, womanly friendship. Rylla found herself telling Jacques some of this.

'But there is—no one else?'

'No.' Stupid, she told herself immediately. You should tell him about Colin. This was the ideal opportunity. But she found she didn't want to talk about Colin Philby to Jacques.

'But, *ma chère*, they are elderly, your aunt and your father. They will not live for ever,' he pointed out gently, though Rylla considered him unnecessarily morbid. 'Doubtless your brother will marry some day. You should have someone of your own. What of the future? Marriage? To Irving, *peut-être*?'

'I'd like to marry some day, of course. But not yet.'

'You are a dedicated career woman?'

'To the extent that I'm not ready to give it up yet.'

'And children? What of them?'

'Perhaps.'

'Do you not think they are the natural outcome of the love between a man and a woman?'

Rylla was growing uncomfortable with this conversation. It was too personal between virtual strangers.

'You're very inquisitive,' she said evasively. 'I don't cross-question you about . . .'

'But I would be delighted, *ma chère*, to tell you anything you care to know.' He waited with evident hope.

'There's nothing,' she said firmly. 'And if you want us to be friends, I'd rather you confined yourself to . . .'

'To Peruvian topics?' His eyebrow was capable of expressing so many varied emotions. 'On which we do not agree? *Hélàs!*' He heaved an exaggerated sigh. 'Have we *no* common ground on which we may meet, *ma chère* Rylla?'

For some illogical reason, she was reminded of that moment in the bus, in the dark Peruvian night when, only for an instant, there had seemed to be accord between them. But it had only been physical attraction.

'None,' she told him firmly. 'We've been thrown together by our respective professions . . .'

'And also by a bus!' he reminded her, wickedly straightfaced, but she ignored him.

'And that's all we have in common.'

They had left the crowded market-place behind them. Now they passed through poor, grubby-looking streets. The houses were tiny and dismal despite the attempts made to brighten their appearance. There were colourful flowers flourishing on their reed-thatched roofs. Puno was only retrieved from dreary insignificance, Rylla thought, by the lake, for which it served as a port.

Titicaca was vast, sensationally beautiful, a shining sheet of water, its surface apparently undisturbed by the fleet of *balsas*, fishing-boats. Snow-capped peaks enclosed the lake, their reflections broken only by a vivid splash of pink where flamingoes waded and fished by the shoreline. This scene aroused all Rylla's professional instincts, and for a while she was occupied with light meter and camera settings.

'The Aymara Indians believe the lake is of divine origin,' Jacques said. He smiled faintly when Rylla forgot her reserve, and in an exquisite moment of aesthetic appreciation turned to him, her delight transforming her normally composed features. '*Eh bien, ma chère!*' he remarked, the blue eyes thoughtful, his tone admiring, 'but you should smile more often.'

Confused, she muttered something unintelligible and turned away in search of the others. Her brother and Irving were deep in conversation with a grave-faced Indian. Jeni stood a little apart from them, and Rylla thought the other woman looked far from well. Moved by her wan appearance, she forgot Jeni's hostile manner towards her and made concerned enquires. Perhaps because of Jacques' presence, Jeni answered civilly enough, albeit unwillingly, that she was suffering from a blinding headache and nausea.

'Altitude sickness,' Jacques diagnosed positively.

'Oh, no!' Jeni protested, too quickly, Rylla thought. 'I'm sure it's just migraine. I . . .'

'You must rest, *ma petite.*' Jacques was unconvinced. 'You know it takes time to become accustomed to altitude. Come, I will take you back to the bus. Rylla, you will explain to Irving, *non?*'

'Oh—yes. Yes, of course.' She watched them walk slowly away from her. Jacques' arm was about Jeni's slight waist. His great height towered protectively over the small woman.

The sight of this solicitude, which until now he had extended only to herself, caused a curious burning sensation in Rylla's breast. Don't be ridiculous, she adjured herself. There was no reason why Jacques shouldn't treat Jeni with equal courtesy. He might receive more response from Jeni than she'd give him, she acknowledged with a ruefulness tinged with an absurd feeling of regret. Perhaps if she continued to rebuff his efforts to flirt, Jacques would transfer his attentions to Jeni Grayson completely. She knew this idea should have pleased her. But instead she felt a vague, inconsistent sensation of chagrin. Impatiently, she brushed these thoughts aside as she moved to join Irving Wilder and Andy.

'Rylla, love, Jacques found you! Come and meet Angel, our guide. Though I'm afraid you won't be able to understand a word he says. He speaks a little Spanish, but mainly Quechua. Good thing Jacques knows some Quechua. Languages aren't my forté.'

Rylla smiled warmly at the brown-skinned Angel. Unlike the men she had seen in the market-place, his clothes were homespun, his sandals home-cured leather. A wide, pale-coloured hat cast a shadow over the long thin face with its deep-set eyes, craggy nose and chin. She looked forward to taking his photograph. His interesting counten-ance should result in some excellent studies.

'Angel is eager to accompany us,' Irving said as he and Rylla strolled back to the bus. 'He believes he's directly descended from the Incas. With those looks of his, he could be right. Now, what's this about Jeni not feeling too good?'

In fact, the other woman looked worse than she had earlier, Rylla thought. Jacques had adminis-tered aspirin and made her get into her sleeping-bag. He told them she had been alternately gasping for air and convulsed with violent retching.

'Maybe we should make her chew coca leaves,' Andy suggested. 'The Indians in high altitudes use it.'

Jacques ignored Andy's flippant manner.

'One thing is certain, we cannot move on until Jeni is recovered.'

'Then we'll make camp by the lake for a day or two,' Irving suggested. 'On Angel's land. The girls can sleep in the bus. Jeni had better not be on her own. OK by you, Rylla?'

'Of course,' she said instantly. She'd never been troubled by altitude sickness herself. But it seemed to be a horrible experience, and she felt extremely sorry for the older woman's wretched state.

'Go on! Say it!' Jeni muttered later as they settled down for the night. Outside, the men's voices were a low murmur as they crawled into their lightweight individual tents. 'You can get your own back now, can't you? I know what you're thinking. *I'm* the one who's holding things up. *I'm* the weak link.' The older woman sounded ineffably weary.

'Don't be silly,' Rylla said at once. 'I wasn't thinking anything of the sort. It could have happened to any of us. It's just bad luck.' She added, 'If you feel rotten again in the night, don't hesitate to wake me up. I sleep like a log.'

'I'd noticed,' Jeni said wryly. Then, as if she found it difficult to make the admission, 'You're a good sort, Rylla. I haven't been very pleasant to you. I'm sorry about that.'

'Oh!' Rylla was embarrassed. 'It doesn't matter. Antagonism *can* arise between expedition members. Sometimes for no particular reason.'

'But it does matter,' Jeni insisted. 'I guess I'd made up my mind not to like you before I met you. Irving was always singing your praises to me and Jacques. About your beauty, your brains. He seems to be very fond of you.'

'Is that all?' Rylla laughed, relieved to find the cause of Jeni's hostility was so slight. 'Irving and I are old friends, and I suppose friends are always inclined to be partial. I'm nothing special. I know what I'm doing where photography is concerned, but as far as this kind of expedition goes . . . In fact,

last year I was a real Johnny-raw. Dad and Irving
were always pulling me out of scrapes. But I'm
glad you told me, Jeni. Now perhaps we can be
friends?'

'Yes, perhaps.' Jeni's response was less than
enthusiastic. But Rylla put it down to the other
woman's continuing malaise. For her own part she
began to feel more cheerful about the weeks
ahead. As the only women on the expedition, she
and Jeni were bound to be thrown together for
some of the time. Perhaps now Jeni knew she had
no cause for professional jealousy ...

'At least this delay will give you a chance to see
more of Puno,' Irving told Rylla next morning.
But he insisted she must not explore alone. 'I'll
keep our invalid company. I've visited Puno
countless times. Besides, it'll be a good opportunity
to bring my log up to date.' Irving kept meticulous
records, every detail of every expedition.

Rylla, Andy and Jacques went to the Cathedral
first. In contrast with its exquisite baroque façade,
the interior was disappointing, simple and hum-
ble. A reflection, Jacques told them, of the local
Aymara Indian's austere attitude towards
religion.

'I must admit I rather like a little pomp and
circumstance,' Rylla told him. 'Somehow, without
the statues, the candles, and the incense there
seems to be no atmosphere.'

'You are *Catholique*?' he hazarded.

'No. But I like their churches, their rituals.'

Andy preferred ruins to architecture, and he did not relish the Frenchman's company. He made that quite obvious before he finally announced his intention of returning to the marketplace. Rylla was reluctant to be left alone with Jacques. She would have accompanied her brother, except that the Frenchman suggested a visit to the municipal museum. It had, he said by way of inducement, an interesting collection of weapons, shreds of clothing and festal ornaments. These items had been retrieved from the few *chulpas*, burial tombs, not looted by the Spaniards.

'When we find Huacaintiraymi,' Rylla enthused as they bent over glass showcases, 'perhaps there'll be undisturbed *chulpas*?'

'*If* we find it,' Jacques reminded her.

'Anyone would think,' she noted curiously, 'that you didn't want to find the Sacred City. Jacques, is it . . .' she hesitated, 'is it because you don't want my father to be right?' Somehow she didn't want to think of Jacques as being that small-minded.

She was not prepared for the fierce grasp of his hands on her shoulders as he swung her away from the display and turned her to face him. His handsome face was unwontedly stern, its planes and angles more prominent than usual, his brows drawn down. The blue eyes were bleak as they met her surprised indignant gaze. She tried to twist free, but his grip on her was inflexible.

'That is the kind of remark I would have expected from your brother! For the love of God, give me *some* credit, Rylla!' His voice was harsh, reverberating in the solemn silence of the museum. 'Whatever else you may accuse me of, let it not be such pettiness.'

'But I *didn't* accuse you,' she began hurriedly, 'I only . . .'

'*Au contraire!*' he swept on, ignoring her protest. 'No one would be more delighted than I to find such a city. But me, I have learned to keep a sense of proportion. There have been any number of aerial surveys of the forest valleys, and we must be prepared for disappointment.'

'But Dad says there are places where even an aerial photographer can see nothing but trees.' Acute depression gripped Rylla. It was due to Jacques' pessimism, she told herself. It couldn't possibly matter so much that he was angry with her.

'And your father may be right,' Jacques amazed her by saying. 'And, if he is, I shall be only too willing to acknowledge it.'

This concession ought to have lifted the depression, but it didn't. She was more upset by the change in his attitude towards her than she would have supposed possible. Moreover, he was dangerously close to her and the disturbing male scent of him assailed her nostrils. Her stomach lurched crazily as she realised she was out of her depth, drowning in the gaze of those gentian-blue eyes.

'Rylla!' He misunderstood her appalled expres-

sion. He gave her a little shake. 'For God's sake,
stop seeing me as some kind of villain,' he rasped.
In the heat of the moment his accent was more
pronounced.

'But I don't . . .'

'What else am I to suppose? *Eh bien!* Loyalty to
your father is admissable. But to imply that I am so
lacking in professional ethics! *C'est insupportable!*'

'You're misunderstanding me,' she tried again.
'I only . . .'

'Your brother is a very immature young man. I
have ignored his remarks. But from you I had
expected more sense. Perhaps you have both been
too indulged by your family and by Irving.'

'Far from it!' she exclaimed. 'My father and my
aunt were kind but strict with us. Neither of them
believed in spoiling children.'

Matthew in particular had shown little indul-
gence towards childish mischief. He had an
unpredictable temper. Even now his children
were grown up he could still be frighteningly
stern.

'Then perhaps it is *lack* of affection that ails you.
Perhaps this is what you need.' He jerked her
against him and as her eyes widened with alarm
his mouth took hers in a fierce, punishing
possession.

Involuntarily her eyes had closed, but her body
stiffened in rejection. She wasn't to be dominated
by sexual chastisement. But she'd reckoned
without the effect of his endless, engulfing kiss, the

leaping response of her flesh to his touch, to the hardening of his body against hers. Suddenly she went limp, her mouth opening to his. A throbbing ache encompassed her entire being. Her hands crept up around his neck and her fingers entwined themselves in the vital blond mane, an exciting tactile sensation. She urged his head closer. Without warning, all her defences against him switched off, leaving her open to the pulsating pull of pure passion. She scarcely knew what was happening to her as the sensuous waves washed over her and she was dragged deeper into tumultuous waters that threatened to drown all reason. No one had ever kissed her like this, parting her lips with a dangerous sensuality. She tried to break free, but his kiss deepened.

When his lips at last left hers and he held her away from him, she moved her head blindly, seekingly, until she realised the kiss was ended. She opened her dark eyes, hazy with the heat of the desire he had induced. Troubled blue eyes beneath frowning brows returned her gaze.

'*Mon Dieu!*' he muttered. He shook his head, as if to clear it. '*Mon Dieu,* but how you provoke me!'

'*Me?* I provoke *you?*' Her voice came out an octave too high. White-faced and trembling, she realised just what his kiss had done to her. He'd made her want him, *really* want him. Feelings which should have been kept for Colin, but which her boyfriend had never aroused. The realisation brought fear; fear brought anger. She glared up at him. 'How dare you treat me like that? You couldn't get round me by other means, so now you're trying the tough approach.' And she hissed forcefully, 'I hate you!' But she knew her hatred was for her own weakness, her own guilt.

'Then nothing is changed, *n'est-ce pas, ma chère* Rylla?' That insolent eyebrow lifted. He seemed quite unmoved by what, to her, had been a cataclysmic experience.

As he turned on his heel she followed him from the museum, out into the street. The doors banged rudely on the hallowed silence within. They marched through the busy streets. The pace he set left Rylla always two or three steps behind, furiously aware that without his guidance she might not find her way back to their camping site.

'No!' The word came out more like a sob as, for an instant, she managed to draw level with him. 'Nothing is changed.' But she didn't hate him. She never had.

CHAPTER FOUR

'RYLLA! Rylla!' The sound of her name being
called and a loud banging on the side of the bus
woke her from a heavy, unrefreshing slumber.
Her troubled thoughts had made it difficult to fall
asleep the previous night. Groggily, she scrambled
out of her sleeping-bag. She pulled up the window
blinds and glared down at her brother.

'Andy? What on earth . . .?'

'Do you know what time it is, Sis? Have you
forgotten we're going on the lake this morning?
Get a move on.'

'Oh!' Rylla groaned. 'I think you'd better count
me out.' She wasn't sure she could face Jacques this
morning.

'OK.' Andy shrugged. 'If you'll let me use your
camera. Irving wants some shots of the Uros and
their floating islands.' Her brother had hit on the
one sure way of changing her mind.

'No way! When it comes to cameras, you're a
disaster area. Tell Irving I'll be five minutes.'

'He said to dress warmly,' Andy reminded her.

'Will you be all right on your own?' Rylla asked
Jeni as she splashed her face with cold water and
scrambled into jeans and a thick red sweater. She
knew the strong colour suited her vivid dark looks,

and somehow she wanted to look her best this morning.

'Yes, thanks. I'm feeling much better today. Tell Irving I should be able to travel tomorrow. Or tonight, if he prefers it.'

A humorous moment bridged the awkwardness of her encounter with Jacques. For Rylla burst out laughing when she met the three men. She insisted there and then on taking a photograph. On their heads all three wore colourful *chullos*, crocheted stocking-caps with earflaps. But the final laugh was on her, as Irving handed her an identical hat.

'Oh, Irving! Do you want me to look as silly as you do?'

'The Indians wear them as protection against the wind. Titicaca is the world's highest navigable lake. It gets pretty chilly. So put it on. Come on, let's get going.'

But when Rylla passed on Jeni's message, Irving paused in his brisk stride.

'If there's a possibility of us leaving tonight, I'll take it. And in that case,' he said, 'I'd better skip the lake. There are preparations to be made. I want to talk to Angel's eldest brother about food for the next stage of our journey. And I ought to take a look at the engine. It's knocking a bit.' Seeing the disappointment Rylla could not quite hide, he went on, 'But there's no reason why you and Jacques shouldn't . . .'

'Oh, no!' she said too quickly. 'We can't. Not if there's work to be done.'

'It won't take four of us. Andy and I can cope, with Angel's help. Right, Andy?'

'I suppose so.' But, from the expression on his face as he and Irving turned back, it was obvious to Rylla that Andy would rather have formed part of the boating expedition. Her brother wasn't very fond of hard labour. She suspected, too, that his grim looks were also at the idea of her being alone with Jacques.

'You truly do not wish to go on the lake with me, Rylla?' Jacques blue eyes quizzed her. 'Is it that you are afraid?' She knew he wasn't referring to the boat trip. 'There is no need. Yesterday you made your feelings most clear. There will be no repetition.'

'If you mean that,' she said slowly, 'I would like to see the islands.'

'*Parole d'honneur!*'

They had no difficulty finding a skipper willing to take his launch on the lake, even though he would have only two passengers. Rylla wondered how much Jacques had paid him.

The Uros Indians, Jacques told her, lived a painfully primitive existence. The lake was their whole life. They fished it for trout. They snared ducks. They built their frail craft, their huts and the floating islands on which they lived, from the buoyant *totora* reeds that flourished in the shallow fringes of the lake.

'Are there many islands?' she asked, as they stood in the bows of the launch. A stiff breeze whipped their faces, so that she was glad of warm clothes, and even the unglamorous *chullo*.

'Over forty. But most trips go only to Huacava-cani, the largest. Unhappily there are few of the Uros left today. Once they were a proud people. They claimed their tribe to be older than the sun. Yet when the Incas ruled Peru they considered the Uros beneath their notice. So they only exacted a hollow cane filled with lice as their monthly tribute.'

Jacques was as informative as ever. As he had promised, his manner towards her was impeccable. He had no '*ma chères*' for her. And apart from helping her into the launch he kept a polite distance. He *had* behaved badly yesterday, but only because of a misunderstanding. She wondered if he was in a mood to listen to explanations.

'Jacques,' she began tentatively.

'Rylla?' He gave her no help.

'About yesterday . . .' Her voice tailed off as his face hardened.

'The matter is closed. I have given my word, *n'est-ce pas*? It will not happen again.'

'But you don't understand. I . . .'

'Me, I understand very well.' He was suddenly vehement. 'Because I have incurred your father's enmity there is no possibility of friendship, or anything else, between us. *Eh bien!* So be it! *N'importe!*'

But somehow it *did* matter. Swallowing, Rylla moved away from him. She began to take photographs—of the skipper, of the surrounding mountains, of the floating islands they had come to see. But her mind was not entirely on her task, and her usually steady hands trembled. If Jacques was so offended with her, he needn't have brought her out here. It was a relief when they arrived at Huacavacani and their Indian skipper offered to act as their guide. He spoke a quaint mixture of Spanish and pidgin English.

Until she actually set foot on one, Rylla had not quite grasped the principle behind the description 'floating island'. As their guide explained, she realised it was quite literally a floating platform, constructed from layer upon layer of the *totora* reeds. The bottom of the island rotted rapidly so that fresh matting was added constantly from above. The whole thing was far less glamorous than she'd envisaged, including the Uros themselves.

'It's like a zoo!' she exclaimed. 'Instead of chimpanzees held captive by surrounding water, these are human beings. Look, Jacques, people are giving them things, money and fruit, the way they'd feed animals. It's insulting.'

'It is not so bad as it seems,' Jacques reassured her. 'The Uros have always lived so. They are realists. Can you blame them for also being opportunists? They are only doing what is done the world over, rooking the tourist. They have their own kind of self-respect. Their craftwork and woollen goods sell well, cheaper than in Puno.'

'Well, I shall buy a tapestry, then,' Rylla decided. She had already admired the unique, brilliantly coloured works. 'And I shall pay them for any photos I take.'

'*Eh bien!* If you are going shopping, leave it until later.' Rylla thought there was a shade more warmth in Jacques' voice. 'There will be no room for parcels aboard a *balsa*.'

'We're not going on one of those?' Rylla surveyed the fragile, leaf-shaped structure. *Totora* reeds again, she noted, bound with rope.

'Why not? You wish to experience everything, *n'est-ce pas*? And the Indian will charge us for the hire of his raft. So all will benefit.'

Rylla was tempted to ask Jacques what benefit *he* expected to derive from the experience. But, prudently, she decided against it.

'They can't be safe,' she said instead.

'*Mais oui!*' Jacques pointed across the lake. In the distance, a dozen or so similar craft were being poled by their owners. 'Come.' He stepped aboard the tiny primitive craft and held out his hand. There was barely room for two, and Rylla hesitated. 'You have fear?' he asked.

She had, but not of the raft. She was a strong swimmer, so water held no terrors for her. She was afraid of putting her hand in his. But Jacques misunderstood.

'There is no need for alarm,' he assured her.

'The Uros also hate the water. They fear they will die if they fall in. Yet they have confidence in their boats. The air in the reeds keeps them afloat for up to six months.'

With a resigned sigh, she accepted the insistent hand, just for the brief moment it took to step aboard. It was quickly over, but the contact sent an electrical impulse through her veins and the sensation lingered long after he had released her.

Jacques was as proficient with the long pole as any Indian. As he moved in the rhythmic action, she found her gaze riveted to his tall, athletic figure, powerful shoulders and chest. He looked over his shoulder and a sudden engaging smile widened his sensual mouth, crinkling the corners of his eyes.

'You look surprised? I was at your Cambridge University. Many years ago, it is true. But one does not forget punting on the River Cam.' It was the first personal information he'd volunteered. He seemed to be in a suddenly communicative mood. 'I was the first of my family to attend university. My parents made many sacrifices to send me to England. I owe them a great deal.'

'Are your parents still both alive?'

'*Oui*, God be praised. They have a small farm. In Provence. In the valley of the Ardèche.' Affection deepened his voice. 'For me, it is the most beautiful place in France. No matter how far I travel, the most beautiful place on earth. The cottages and farms are washed in pinks, blues and white. The atmosphere is so clear, the light is so brilliant. Sometimes the mountains are brown, sometimes grey. Sometimes they are deep blue or purple, but never twice the same. I think you would like it.'

'Do you go home often?'

'*Hélas*, not as often as I would wish. My work entails much travelling, you understand?'

'Have you any brothers or sisters?'

'One sister only, Simone. She is married and I have two small nephews, Jean-Paul and Pierre.' There was affection in his tone as he spoke of the little boys, and Rylla sensed that he was particularly fond of children. 'My brother-in-law manages the farm. My parents are elderly, you understand? They are retired from physical work.'

She waited for him to tell her about a wife and children. But he said nothing, and somehow she couldn't ask.

'I expect your parents are very proud of you? You're famous.'

'I suppose.' He inclined his fair head. 'But their pride is a quiet, modest one. They are not possessive. They make no demands of me, claim no debts of gratitude.'

For some reason, his words made Rylla think uncomfortably of Matthew. Matthew was a demanding parent. But she pushed the disloyal thought to the back of her mind.

'But you feel a debt?' she suggested. If so, he

should be able to understand her loyalty to Matthew.

'*Naturellement!* And I do my utmost for them. But I am not a rich man.'

'Not?' This was a surprise. She'd always believed him to be extremely wealthy.

'*Mais non!* My books and my lectures earn me a competence. But expeditions are expensive to fund. I am most grateful for this opportunity to accompany Irving on a salaried basis. And you, Rylla? Tell me more about you. Do you live with your father and your aunt?'

'No, he lives in Cheshire. In a lovely old Tudor house that's been in the family for generations.' She grimaced ruefully. 'I'm afraid it's rather expensive to run, which is why Dad isn't too well off, but he won't hear of moving into anything smaller. I have a small flat in London, over my studio and laboratory. It's more convenient.'

'You live alone?'

'Of course.'

'But you have friends?'

'Yes. But I'm away a lot, so they're not very close ones, except for Colin.' Rylla had decided it was time she mentioned Colin Philby's existence.

'And he is a *close* friend, this Colin? Very close?'

'Yes. He'd like to marry me some day.'

'And you? You wish to marry him?'

'Yes.' Something compelled her to be strictly honest. 'At least, I think so.' She waited a little breathlessly for his comment, but he made none and she felt strangely deflated.

They were both silent on the return to Puno. Rylla felt that she'd learned a lot about Jacques. She approved of the way he'd spoken about his parents, his family and his home. And the more she knew of him, the more she found herself liking him. It was a pity, she thought vaguely, but did not complete the thought.

'Machu Picchu!' Andy sounded distinctly aggrieved. 'Again? We were only there the year before last. There won't be anything new. So why?'

'Several reasons, Andy, old son!' Irving never lost his polite patience with anyone, Rylla thought. Not even with Andrew, who could be very trying at times. She gave the older man an affectionate grin and he put an arm about her shoulders. 'The girls haven't been there, for one thing. And I particularly want Rylla to see it. But, apart from that, Machu Picchu plays a vital part in my calculations. You all remember the bearings I took while we were at Nasca? There were two of those *ceques* that might be relevant to Matt's theory.'

Matthew Quarmby believed the Nasca Lines were ley lines, the source of mysterious power, which linked ancient religious sites.

Irving unfolded a large map and spread it out for the others to see.

'Two of those lines, if we extend them east, head

in the right direction.' He indicated a point on the map, just north of their present position. 'I'm almost certain one of them is linked with the Temple of the Sun at Machu Picchu. I want to check that out. Because, if so, I believe the second line will bring us to Molina's lost city.'

As Irving spoke, Rylla watched Jacques. She had expected to see scepticism on his handsome face, but his expression was one of immense interest. He'd been very quiet today. He hadn't spoken much to anyone, and not at all to her. He seemed to feel the intensity of her gaze and turned his head to meet it. At once, a flush of betraying colour flooded her cheeks. She hoped he hadn't misunderstood the reason for her close scrutiny. Not now they had agreed to a purely professional working relationship.

'Machu Picchu!' Rylla said on a note of awe. Photographs had given her only the merest taste of the reality. Even the fact that they were not the only visitors could not spoil it. For the ruins were swarmed with tourists, like minute ants on a vast sculptured ant-hill.

Until now, Machu Picchu, the as yet unrivalled fortress of the Incas, had been only a name to her. The site was protected by mountains and a wide gorge, through which foamed a turbulent river. No wonder the *conquistadores* had never discovered it. It was part of Inca genius to seal themselves into concealed valleys. She hoped Huacaintiraymi would prove as excitingly substantial when they found it. She still had no doubt that they would.

Forty-eight hours had passed since their voyage on Lake Titicaca. In the benign air of warmer valleys, Jeni's improvement had been rapid. But Jacques still maintained a solicitous care of the other woman. He treated Rylla with rigorous politeness. Well, that was what she'd wanted, wasn't it?

Because of the height, ten thousand feet above the gorge, Jeni decided not to make the steep, winding climb which soon had rivulets of perspiration running down Rylla's back.

'I can't get over the size of it!' Rylla gasped aloud as she paused to catch her breath. Irving and Andy were striding on ahead and she thought she was alone.

'Two hundred and fifty buildings. All of them hewn out of the mountainside,' Jacques' husky voice sounded in her ear. 'There are a hundred staircases and three thousand steps.' It was the first time in forty-eight hours that he'd addressed her directly, and he still sounded coolly impersonal. But Rylla found herself grateful for any concession.

'How on earth did they construct such massive buildings?'

'Incredible, is it not? They had no draught animals, no wheeled vehicles. Only the most primitive of tools.'

Yet the Incas had managed to split the huge

granite blocks, then haul them up deep gorges to sites sometimes miles away. They'd had no mortar, Jacques told her, yet, and he demonstrated, the stones were fitted together so tightly that it was impossible even now to insert a knife-blade between them.

'Jacques! Rylla! Look at this!'

Irving beckoned from one of the upper terraces. By the time they reached him Rylla's legs were aching, her clothes sticking to her body. Irving was standing by a circular stone pillar over six foot high. When they reached him he was using his calculator. His brown eyes glowed triumphantly.

'Dead on! One *ceque* aligns exactly with this spot. Do you know what this is, Rylla?' And, before she could answer, 'Lift her up, Jacques, so she can see.'

'No, that isn't necessary——' Rylla began; but the Frenchman had already clasped his arms around her waist. He lifted her so her face was on a level with the curved *stele*, stone tablet, that rose from the centre of the pillar. 'A sundial!' she exclaimed. Then, 'You can put me down now,' she told Jacques rather breathlessly.

He did so, but with a lingering slowness that jangled her nerves. She turned indignantly to protest, but as she caught his eye she thought better of it. Jacques knew exactly what effect he'd had on her. Moreover, she sensed he was not unaffected himself. One of his hands would have remained at her waist had she not edged away from him. Too late, she realised the reason for the restraining hand. Her sideways movement had brought her to the terrace edge and she only just avoided a nasty fall, but at the expense of her ankle. Pain contorted her face as she sank to the ground.

'*Mon Dieu!*' Jacques reached her first. He sounded disproportionately angry.

'Rylla, you idiot!' was all the sympathy her brother gave her. 'If you've broken anything, bang goes your trip! And don't expect *me* to take you home.'

'If she's broken anything, *someone* will have to take her back to Lima,' Irving said worriedly.

While they exclaimed, Jacques removed Rylla's sock and shoe. He was gentle as he examined the damaged ankle. But even so she winced with pain.

'You are more fortunate than you deserve,' he told her grimly. 'It is just a sprain. Not a bad one. But it is beginning to swell. You will never make it back to the bus unaided. One of us must carry you.'

'Irving . . .' Rylla began.

'*Ciel!* Do you want to give him a heart attack? He is a much older man. He is finding the altitude punishing enough.' Jacques gave her no chance for argument or resistance. He swung her up against the hard strength of his shoulder and started back down the steep track. Her nerves screamed a warning message as she felt the warmth of him through her thin shirt, heard his heart pounding beneath her ear. With a shock of dismay she found herself imagining Jacques' touch on her bare skin.

'Damn! Damn! Damn!' Rylla was disappointed at having her visit to the famous city curtailed. But she exaggerated her annoyance. It was better than having Jacques guess the real reason why she was trembling. 'I wanted to see the temples.'

'There will be more temples,' he said shortly. 'If you can manage to refrain from injuring yourself.'

'Goodness! Whatever happened to you?' Jeni asked as they reached the bottom of the steep track and Jacques set her down.

'I fell,' Rylla said shortly. She was still fighting for self-control. 'After all that effort, all I got to see was a measly sundial.'

'But no ordinary sundial,' Jacques said. 'That was the *Intihuatana*, Stone of the Sun. The Incas believed that the sun was tethered to it by magic. If we find our city, there should be an identical stone outside its main temple.' As he spoke, he knelt at Rylla's feet, crêpe bandage in hand.

'I can do that myself,' she protested.

'It was being so independent that caused your injury,' Jacques reproved her.

'Yes, you're right,' she said with a meekness that surprised her. And Jacques gave her a sharp, penetrating glance. Her ankle was extremely painful, she excused herself. But she felt ashamed of the tears that suddenly blurred her eyes. To her

horror, she felt one spill over. Her hasty attempt to
brush it away betrayed her.

'*Tant pis, ma chère!*' It seemed ages since he'd
called her that. And she'd missed the affectionate
words. A large hand, which she'd discovered could
also be gentle, cupped her cheek. A thumb
brushed away a second tear. As her lower lip
quivered ominously, he asked, 'Is it the pain?'

'Yes. But it's not just that. I could have ruined
everything, for everyone.' It *was* the realisation of
her own foolishness which was making her feel so
low, she told herself fiercely. But, oh, she was glad
Jacques was being nice to her again!

Jacques took one of her hands in both of his.

'Have no fear, *ma chère*. All will be well,' he said,
somewhat ambiguously. Hazily she wished it
could be, but wasn't sure what she meant.

Encouraged by their fifty-per-cent success, Irving
was eager to press on.

'It's not far now till we turn off the known road.
The time will come when we'll have to leave the
bus. We'll have to go on foot then. Or horseback, if
we're lucky.'

Rylla hoped fervently that there would be
horses available. By the next day her ankle was
much improved. But it wasn't strong enough for
prolonged walking; and she knew the jungle
terrain would be very varied.

After they left the main highway, an adequate
road continued for some distance over a plateau.

Gradually the road deteriorated until it became little more than a track encroached upon by vividly coloured vegetation. The bus's springs groaned as they lurched over hard-baked mud. The only person who seemed to be enjoying the ride was Angel. He sat up in front with Irving and Jacques, chattering in his mixture of pidgin English, Spanish and Quechua, which only the Frenchman understood. Jacques seemed to speak the sweet, flexible, rhythmic tongue as easily as his own native French.

'*Eh bien, mes amis!*' he shouted above the vehicle's noise, 'Angel has been here before. He tells me there is a village ahead. It may be a suitable place to leave the bus.'

At first sight, the hamlet on the jungle edge looked disappointingly derelict. But, as the bus shuddered to a halt, figures emerged from the rectangular adobe buildings.

Angel conversed with the villagers. Jacques made an occasional contribution, and translated for the benefit of the others.

'They can provide ponies. One of their men will accompany us to look after the animals. We can make camp for the night, and the bus can be left here until we return.'

'Will it be safe?' Rylla asked.

'*Mais oui.* They will regard it as a sacred trust for those who go to the "City of the Gods".'

'They've heard of the city? Oh, Jacques! That means it must exist.'

'*Doucement, ma chère!*' Jacques laughed gently at her eagerness. 'If we foreigners have heard rumours, why not these people?'

There was enough daylight left for photography. The villagers seemed anxious to please. They posed for her and invited her into their one-roomed, windowless houses. The only door was a draped curtain and there were no chimneys. Smoke was left to find its own way out and the atmosphere beneath the thickly thatched roofs made her eyes smart.

They shared the villagers' evening meal, which consisted mainly of corn, and Andy's wry face-pulling amused his companions.

The two girls spent a last night in the bus.

'Make the most of it,' Irving told them. 'From now on, it's sleeping-bags and jungle hammocks.'

Rylla had not seen any horses about the village, but next morning there were nine sturdy ponies waiting for them, two of them pack animals to carry provisions and equipment. They set off in single file.

Quickly, imperceptibly, the jungle was upon them. It was a revelation to Rylla to find the trees such a fantastic height. Trees, creepers, everything reached upwards, vainly seeking the sunlight. The warm air swiftly became moist, heavy and oppressive. Always imaginative, Rylla had the sensation of entering an alien world where they were not welcome. The atmosphere seemed to demand silence, and they spoke little. Except when a twig snapped or a pony's hoof dislodged a stone, they made no sound on the damp earth.

Hours passed as they penetrated further into the jungle. A light, misty rain began to fall, though the umbrella-like foliage above gave them some protection. Even the air had a green haze, for very little light penetrated the dense growth.

'I thought this was supposed to be the dry season,' Rylla said.

'It is,' Jacques agreed, 'but the weather in Peru is as eccentric as anywhere else in the world.'

The next day the flies came. The insects had long proboscises with biting stings. And, even though the two girls had smothered their tender hands and faces with repellent cream, the flies seemed not to be deterred.

They stopped at intervals so that the men could dismount and examine the jungle floor. Rylla noticed that this always happened where the going was soft and marshy.

'What are you looking for?' she asked Jacques a little anxiously. The procedure reminded her of big game hunters tracking wild beasts.

'We're looking for signs that the road ran this way. The technical term for it, if you're interested, is the *agger*.'

'Are you likely to find anything after all these years?'

'Maybe, maybe not. It would be a useful confirmation that we are on the right track.'

A few hours later, Irving gave an exultant shout.

'This is stone—paving stone! There *has* been a road here once.'

Immediately the others surrounded him. They scraped away moss and undergrowth, and uncovered yet another huge stone, enough to satisfy Irving that they had found part of the road they sought.

'Photograph, please, Rylla!' he requested.

From then on, their progress became even slower. They had to halt frequently to make sure they were still following the road. This meant a lot of digging. Over the centuries the ancient highway had been almost completely obliterated.

'We are searching for a distinct pattern,' Jacques told Rylla as they worked harmoniously, side by side. 'Molina described a road with steps and resting places running through spectacular scenery. There would have been storehouses and temples. The standard width would have been between fifteen and eighteen feet, but not necessarily paved for its entire length. Often stone was only used for causeways in waterlogged areas.'

Further on they came across remains which Irving decided must be a former resting station.

Rylla was disappointed.

'I don't see how you can tell.' It seemed hardly worthwhile photographing the few large, irregularly shaped stones. But as each day brought more and more evidence to light, she realised that they were making good progess, that their finds had all the hallmarks of Inca work.

Day after day the track continued, always with the familiar bordering stones. Then Rylla stumbled across the remains of a drainage system. Exuberantly, Irving shook hands with the men. But he swung both girls off their feet in a bone-crushing hug.

'Clever girl, Rylla!'

As he set her back on her feet, she caught Jacques' quizzical eyes upon them and flushed. But she felt vaguely hurt when his congratulations were quietly understated.

'Damn! I knew things were going too smoothly,' Irving said exasperatedly a day or two later. They had come to a point where the road forked in two different directions. 'One's probably a "feed" road to a resting station. Most likely it will peter out after a few miles. But which one do we take?'

'So, now what?' Jeni asked.

'Well, we don't want to follow a track only to discover it's a dead end.'

'If I may suggest,' Jacques said, 'we could divide into two groups. The party that finds itself on the wrong track could return to this point and follow the others.'

'How do we split up?' Andy asked. Rylla had been wondering that, too.

'I'll head one group,' Irving said, 'Jacques, the

other. Angel had better go with Jacques. He understands his lingo. So that means Andy goes with me and we take a girl apiece.'

'Can I go with you, Irving?' Jeni asked quickly.

Rylla was surprised. She would have expected Jeni to prefer the Frenchman's company.

'*Eh bien*, Rylla!' Jacques said in a quiet aside, a hint of mischief lurking in his blue eyes. 'Do you still not believe in fate?'

'No.' But she had to restrain a smile. 'I believe in what I can see, touch and hear. Fate doesn't come into any of those categories.'

'*C'est vrai?*' He feigned astonishment. 'Yet you are prepared to support your father's theories against mine. Without any tangible proof.'

'That's faith, not fate,' Rylla quipped. 'A very different thing.'

But as the party divided she was beginning to wonder if there wasn't some unseen agency at work.

'You would rather have accompanied Irving?' Jacques asked.

'I don't mind, either way.' It would have been safer to go with Irving, but she'd wanted to accompany Jacques, she realised.

The jungle was too dense now for the ponies. The animals were left behind with the villager, Corchuelo, who promised to await their return. From now on, they would carry their own supplies on their backs. Rylla was grateful that the days on horseback had rested her ankle. She was going to need all her strength in the days that lay ahead.

The first drops of rain began to fall as, Angel leading, they toiled up a steep track which led to and then ran alongside the white-flecked course of a waterway, much swollen by rain. Rylla thanked heaven for waterproof camera cases!

It was a nightmarish journey over the slippery ground, and she was very aware of Jacques following close behind her. She was anxious not to take a false step on the precarious footing. She didn't want to precipitate herself into his arms yet again. She found herself smiling; that would be stretching the hand of fate too far.

The rain was more than a downpour now. It was a prolonged cascade that formed puddles inches deep in their pathway and that soaked them to the skin, despite their waterproof clothing. The track was inches deep in liquid mud and water. Wind stirred the treetops, lashing them into frenzied movement. The temperature had fallen and Rylla's teeth chattered. The leaden sky and icy wind kept them moving fast and, just as she thought conditions could scarcely get worse, thunder rolled menacingly overhead.

'We must find cover before dark,' Jacques warned, 'or we run the risk of hypothermia. I did tell you the going would be hard, *ma chère*.'

Rylla thought he looked anxious. He was probably worried about her becoming a liability. She set her teeth. That wouldn't happen.

'I'll manage.'

But it took all her courage to keep going. She
followed in Jacques' wake now. She was too tired,
too hot and too wet to be curious about the noise
that seemed to shake the earth beneath their feet.
The track wound steeply down into a culvert and
she saw the cause of the disturbance. The river was
now a roaring torrent, a boiling, swirling mass of
brown foam. On its far side, a cliff rose dizzily.
Lightning licked the wet rockface and Angel
paused to consult the Frenchman. There was
much gesturing and head-shaking before Jacques
turned to Rylla.

'The road stops at the river's edge. There may
have been a bridge or a ford once. Angel believes
there may be caves in the cliff-face where we can
shelter. But it means we have to cross the river.'
Rylla must have looked dismayed, for he went on,
'It is the only way, *ma chère*. There is no cover this
side. To spend a night in the open would mean
certain death.'

'Drowning's a pretty certain way of dying, too,'
Rylla said, with a wry attempt at humour. She
looked at the turbulent water. She was a strong
swimmer, but this was no gently swelling sea.

'Me, I will not let you drown. *Parole d'honneur!*'
He'd given his word before and kept it, but in
very different circumstances. They removed their
boots. Jacques insisted on hanging both pairs
around his neck, together with Rylla's cameras.
He made her give her knapsack to Angel, then
held out his hand to her. She made a gallant

attempt to hide her fear at the plunge they were about to take.

Angel led the way, and they entered the ice-cold river. At once the water was up to their thighs. Instinctively, Rylla tightened her grasp on Jacques's hand. The force of the current dragged at their legs, threatening to overbalance them. Forward progress was slow. The noise of the rushing water made it impossible to hear Jacques' mouthed words of encouragement. It was a living nightmare.

As they reached the centre of the torrent, when the far bank was just a black outline in the deepening gloom, disaster struck. A dip in the riverbed made it suddenly deeper. Jacques stumbled, Rylla lost her balance. She floundered out of her depth. The shock of the icy water engulfing her up to her chin made her gasp for breath. Then the black, numbing waters closed over her head.

CHAPTER FIVE

'RYLLA! Rylla, *ma chère!*'

Choking, coughing, shivering, Rylla came up out of the blackness. She was in the shallows of the opposite bank. Jacques' arm was a vice about her waist. With him urging her on, she clawed at the foliage and scrambled on all fours up the muddy incline. As she felt her feet touch firm ground, Rylla turned to look for their guide. There was no sign of him.

Between chattering teeth, she asked, 'Where's Angel?'

In the almost darkness, she sensed rather than saw Jacques shrug.

'Swept away downriver, I'm afraid, poor devil!'

'Oh, my God! We must find him.' She started off in the direction he'd indicated, but he caught her arm and dragged her back.

'Impossible! It is too dark. We do not know the terrain.'

'But we can't just leave him to drown,' she sobbed. 'Wasn't there anything you could do? Don't you care?'

'Of course I care,' he said roughly, 'but by the time I had brought you across he was gone.'

'If he hadn't been carrying my knapsack, as well as his own, he might have made it. I could have managed my own things somehow.' But she knew she couldn't. She was a good swimmer, but her skills would have been useless against the raging current. It had taken all Jacques' physical strength and determination to get them both across the river. He had saved her life and she was glad to be alive. But she would never be able to forget that Angel's life had been the price of hers. She shivered. A combination of wet, cold and nervous reaction.

'We must keep moving,' Jacques said. 'We must find shelter and dry out.'

'But what about poor Angel?' Sobs racked her. 'How are we going to tell his family, his wife?'

'Come, *ma chère*,' Jacques' voice was resonant with feeling. 'Angel is in the hands of God. But you are my responsibility. I promised Irving I would look after you.'

The ordeal, the shock of Angel's disappearance had sapped all the strength from Rylla's legs. She sagged suddenly, and only Jacques' lightning reflexes prevented her from slumping to the ground. Dimly, she was aware of being swung aloft in strong arms, before everything became a blur.

She was propped against a rough, hard, unyielding surface. She couldn't see a thing, and for a moment she panicked.

'Jacques?'

'*Restes tranquille, ma chère*. I am here.' By the light of a torch she saw the interior of a cave. Jacques was kneeling a few feet away. His waterproof knapsack was open beside him, and he pulled out a towel. 'Take off those wet clothes,' he ordered.

'Oh, no, I . . .'

'*Mais oui!*' he said firmly. 'This is no time for modesty. Unless you wish to be dead by morning.' He moved the beam of the torch around the cave. 'Someone has used this place in the past. There is dry kindling. I will light a fire to dry our clothes.'

Rylla's spare kit had been in the knapsack lost with Angel. The thought brought fresh distress for the young Indian. Helplessly she shook her head from side to side. She was too weary and dispirited to make any effort. With a muttered imprecation, Jacques moved to her side. His fingers dealt efficiently with the buttons of her shirt, the zip of her jeans.

'No, please, don't,' she begged weakly. But there was no strength in the hands that tried to ward him off. When only her bra and panties remained, he handed her the towel.

'You can dry yourself,' he commanded gruffly. 'For I am only flesh and blood, *ma chère* Rylla.'

She flushed as she realised he was referring to the effect upon him of undressing her. Galvanised into action, she rubbed briskly at her damp body then wrapped herself in the towel.

Within minutes Jacques had a fire burning near the entrance to the cave. Then, quite unselfcon-

sciously, he began to strip off his own clothes.
Rylla had suspected that Jacques had a magnificent body. Now, in the flickering firelight, it was
revealed to her. The muscular chest that tapered
down to a firm waist, the flat stomach and . . . She
knew she ought to look away, but she couldn't. He
was magnificent. She swallowed nervously as he
moved towards her.

'I regret, but I must trouble you for the use of
the towel.'

'Oh—of course.' She lowered her eyes as she
handed it to him.

To do so meant losing its scanty protection, and
she felt his gaze travel over her near-naked
loveliness. He was inches away, yet it was as if he
were touching her. Her skin tingled. She knew she
ought to move away. But it was as if invisible
chains held her. He put a hand on her arm. The
touch was like an electric current running
through her. She caught her breath in an audible
gasp.

'You're trembling,' he murmured.

'Yes. It's cold.'

'I have put the sleeping-bag near the fire. Please
get into it.'

She obeyed, glad of anything that would hide
her from his eyes. So she was horrified when a
moment later he began to scramble in beside her.

'What are you doing?' she squeaked.

'Perhaps you didn't realise, *ma chère*,' he said
drily, 'but unfortunately this is the only protection

we have. This, and each other's warmth.' It was *his*
sleeping-bag. Hers was somewhere down river
with the unfortunate Angel. But it wasn't only
that thought that made her shudder as his large
body eased in alongside her.

This was a new experience for Rylla. She had
never shared a room before, let alone a bed. Some
of her friends slept with their boyfriends, but
Colin had never suggested it. Even if he had, she
would never have allowed their relationship to go
that far. Not before marriage. That was for the
man with whom you hoped to spend the rest of
your life.

It was a large sleeping-bag. For two people of
slight build it might have been adequate. But both
Rylla and Jacques were generously built.

'I—I don't think this is a good idea.' Every
nerve in her body was taut and screaming at his
proximity. She attempted to struggle free, but in
the tightly enclosed space her efforts brought her
into closer contact with the warmth and hardness
of his body.

'Be still!' he growled warningly. 'Or I will not
be responsible for the consequences.'

She couldn't misunderstand him. She'd felt his
body go rigid as she brushed against him.

'Turn your back towards me. Lie on your side,'
he ordered.

She obeyed. But he turned with her, his body
curving around hers, and she felt she'd gained
nothing by the manoeuvre. She was vibrantly

aware of him, all the more for having seen the
stirring perfection of his naked maleness. For a
moment she let herself imagine his mouth on hers,
remember the whole lean length of his muscular
body. But when a heavy arm curved around her
waist she stiffened.

'Jacques! Please don't!'

He removed his arm and was silent for a
moment, then he said wryly, 'You are right. But
we have been through so much together tonight,
ma chère. Do you not feel it has brought us closer
together?'

'You could have experienced the same dangers
with another man,' she argued. 'Just because I'm a
woman doesn't mean . . .'

'That I have to make love to you? That is what
you fear?'

'Yes. No. I mean . . .' Rylla became incoherent.
'I don't want you to think . . . Just because we have
to share a sleeping-bag. And it wouldn't be love. It
would be . . .'

'Would you like it to be love?' he asked
throatily.

'No!' The word was a strangled sound in her
throat. But she was ashamed at the tide of warmth,
the swift intimate ache of longing that engulfed
her. 'Jacques, I've never . . . I've never been to bed
with a man.'

There was a long silence.

'D-don't you believe me?'

'Oh, yes.' It was a long, sighing sound. 'I believe

you.' A pause, then, 'Goodnight, Rylla.'

Long after his steady breathing told her he was asleep, Rylla was wide awake. She'd tried so hard these past few weeks to think of Jacques just as a colleague. But it had become impossible to ignore his effect on her. His proximity now was a searing torment. She wanted him. And she knew it was nothing new that she acknowledged. It was something inevitable that she'd fought against since their first meeting in Lima. Jacques wanted her. She knew that, too. But it wasn't love. They were only human, both of them. The danger they'd gone through together had brought out the primitive element in both of them. She tried desperately to distract her thoughts by going over the events of the day. But these had culminated in the loss of their guide.

Such a good-natured, willing man. Too young to lose his life. She knew tiredness was increasing her depression, that spirits were always at their lowest ebb at night, that it wasn't just the thought of Angel's death that ailed her. But she couldn't prevent the shuddering sob that shook her from head to foot.

'*Qu'est-ce que c'est?*' Jacques' hand on her shoulder was a gentle enquiry.

'I'm sorry. I didn't mean to wake you. But I keep thinking about poor Angel. Such a dreadful thing to be drowned like that. And he was so far from home. If we hadn't asked him to be our guide, he'd still be alive. We can't even take his body back for burial.' Her voice wavered and became indistinct as fresh tears choked her.

'Would it help, *chérie*, if I held you?' And, as she didn't answer, 'There would be nothing more, *ma chère*.'

It seemed natural to turn into the comforting strength of Jacques' arms. She pressed her wet face to the rough warmth of his chest and felt his hand move soothingly at the nape of her neck.

'You have a compassionate nature, *ma chère*. A warm, loving nature. You are a woman formed to love and be loved.' At the sensuous words, she shuddered. 'And you are still cold. Let me warm you,' he said huskily.

The kiss was inevitable. His hands on her naked flesh were a delight. Sensual warmth drove away the chill of misery as her body came alive to his touch. They clung together and she felt his deep arousal.

She wanted him to make love to her. She wanted him as she'd never wanted any man before. He would be her first lover, and all her instincts told her Jacques would be a wonderful lover.

She moved closer to him and slid her hands around his neck, her fingers entwined in the long hair at the nape of his neck. Again and again their lips met.

And he wanted her as much as she wanted him. She was sure of that. His arms were tight about her, his body excitingly hard against hers.

'Love me, Jacques!'

But with a sense of shock she realised he was moving away from her.

'No, Rylla!' he exclaimed. But despite the words she sensed the effort cost him dearly.

'Jacques?' She couldn't understand his sudden withdrawal.

'Ironic, isn't it?' he said almost savagely, 'that I should have promised Irving I'd take care of you? And then for a moment I almost . . .' He scrambled from the sleeping-bag and rummaged in his haversack. Almost violently he flung one of his spare shirts at her. 'Put that on.' He was pulling on his wet trousers again. And when he returned he held himself as far away from her as the dimensions of the sleeping-bag would permit.

'Go to sleep, Rylla,' he said roughly.

A shaft of sunlight stabbed through the entrance to the cave, waking Rylla. For a moment she lay in heavy-eyed confusion. Then the events of the past day and night rushed in upon her. With an incoherent little cry she turned to seek the reassurance of Jacques' presence. But he was no longer there.

She sat up. The cave was empty. The fire had burned down to grey ashes. Jacques' clothes had gone and outside it was full daylight. She scrambled out of the sleeping-bag, slipped out of the shirt which was far too large for her and, clad only in her scanty underwear, she ran to the entrance of the cave. She paused, catching her breath at the scene before her.

However had Jacques managed to climb up the perilous way last night, carrying her in his arms? The steep track was only inches wide, and the cliff-face fell away sheer to the river valley below. It had stopped raining and the watercourse had subsided a little. But its current was still strong and she shuddered, remembering that instant when she'd been sure she would drown.

Sunlight glittered on every wet leaf, wild pigeons cooroo'd and countless unseen birds trilled a greeting to the new day. But Rylla no longer had eyes or ears for her surroundings. Where was Jacques? He wouldn't abandon her. He had promised Irving he would take care of her. And after last night she knew she could trust him—with her life, and more besides. This morning she felt ashamed and embarrassed by her own wanton behaviour. She'd offered herself to a man. She had never done such a thing before in her life. But she had been at a low ebb physically and mentally, she excused herself. It would have been very easy for Jacques to have taken advantage of her. But he hadn't.

Then she saw him on the river's edge, walking upstream. And a sudden upsurge of joy expanded within her until she thought her heart would burst with its force. It wasn't just relief. She was unutterably glad to see him. In that moment she knew just how important he had become to her.

She began to make her way down the steep track
to meet him.

All her concentration was needed for the
narrow way, and it was not until she reached the
valley floor that she realised Jacques was not
alone. Then, with a little cry of gladness, she ran
towards the two men.

'It's Angel! He's alive. What happened? Where
did you find him?'

At her impetuous rush, Jacques' arms closed
about her. For a brief moment he held her tightly,
staring down into her glowing face. Then, with a
laugh he said, 'All in good time, *chérie*. I think you
are embarrassing our good Angel. And as to your
effect upon me!' He drew in a breath and she saw a
muscle leap in his jaw.

It was only then that Rylla realised she'd run to
meet Jacques just as she was, in bra and panties.
But Angel didn't seem particularly embarrassed.
He regarded her with a cheerful admiring grin.
And Jacques? The deep awareness in those
gentian-blue eyes, the familiar lift of his eyebrow,
made her cheeks colour hotly, made her sharply
conscious of him.

'I forgot I wasn't . . . I was so pleased to see you.'

'Did you think I had abandoned you, *ma chère*?'
He threw down a knapsack which she recognised
as her own, and pulled out her spare shirt and
jeans.

'No, I didn't think you'd do that,' she said as she
scrambled into the clothes. 'But I was afraid

something had happened to you.'

'*C'est vrai?*' There was a curious note in his voice. 'You would care?'

'Of course,' she said indignantly. 'You saw how upset I was about Angel.' But she knew the loss of Jacques would have meant far more to her.'

'Ah, of course.' There could have been a note of chagrin in Jacques' voice. Rylla wasn't certain.

'Tell me about Angel,' she demanded as they reascended the cliff-face.

'The current carried him downstream, where he was able to scramble ashore and take shelter. He knew he would never find us in the dark, I went out early this morning, thinking to find his body. *Et voilà*, we met.'

Inside the cave she turned to him. Impulsively she set a hand on his arm.

'Jacques, I want to thank you. Oh, not just for saving my life, but for last night, too.' Because her eyes were shyly downcast, she did not see the quizzical look in his.

'For last night?' he prompted gently. 'But, *ma chère*, I did nothing.'

'That's what I want to thank you for.' She ventured to look up, saw his expression looked away again and became incoherent. 'I behaved very stupidly and you could have ... I mean, if you'd been a different kind of man.'

'I am "different" to the men you have known before?' His voice sounded oddly strangled and she had a notion he was restraining mirth.

'It was meant as a compliment,' she assured him. He moved closer and she felt a shivering excitement.

'Rylla!' His voice was husky. 'Look at me.'

'Jacques, I . . .' He stretched out a large hand and tilted up her chin. 'Please, don't,' she begged.

'I would never do anything to hurt you,' he murmured. He bent his head and his lips touched her brow in a featherlight kiss.

Instinctively her eyes closed. She felt her body go soft and pliant as his free hand drew her to him. Then his mouth was on hers. Not demanding, nor teasing, but gently sweet. The kiss was achingly sensuous, causing a delicious warmth to spread through her body. Then both arms held her, drawing her tightly up against him, and he buried his face in her hair. But, just as she was wishing this moment could last for ever, he released her.

'Angel will be wondering what's keeping us.' He cleared a throat grown strangely hoarse. 'It's time to move on, *ma chère*. You feel able to do so?'

'Of course.' She'd felt strangely bereft as he put her away from him. But she swallowed her disappointment. 'What now?'

An arm about her shoulders, he steered her out on to the ledge.

'What do you see?'

'Jungle?'

'Look again.' He pointed and then she saw it. The raised contours of the ancient road, running from the riverbank into the jungle. 'We could not have chosen a more ideal spot. At ground level, the *agger* of the old road is invisible.'

'So we're on the right track?' For the moment, excitement overrode all other emotions.

'Another day's march may tell.' Jacques was still cautious.

On this side of the river the jungle was more lush, more impenetrable. Jacques and Angel hacked a way through tangles of creeper and tendril, a parasitic growth that linked the trees in confused trailing masses. Frustrating, clinging, like giant spider's webs. The smell of dank, rotting vegetation was heavy in their nostrils. They floundered on, maintaining direction by compass.

Rylla felt helpless. She was hot and dirty, and there was little she could do to assist the men. In the oppressive heat she could only just support the weight of her knapsack and cameras. She knew she ought to be taking photographs. But she was too busy watching her feet, anxious not to trip over a vine or step on a snake. But Jacques seemed untiring. His ebullience unabated, he pointed out vividly coloured flowers, told her the names of trees.

Once, they disturbed a flock of bright green and yellow birds which flew up suddenly. Rylla was startled into a little cry of alarm. Jacques paused and turned to give her a reassuring smile, and she knew that whatever difficulties they might encounter her fear would be less because of his presence.

They stopped to eat at midday. Angel lit a fire and soon water from their precious store was boiling in the billy can. Into this the Indian stirred powdered vegetables.

'It's not the Ritz, but it'll do,' Rylla said.

'Unless we find a source of food tomorrow, we shall have to ration ourselves,' Jacques told her.

'If we do find food, shall we wait for Irving?'

He shook his blond head decisively.

'*Non*. It would be foolish to waste time and energy. We must either go on or go back.'

'You wouldn't turn back?' she cried in dismay. 'Not when we've come so far?'

'If necessary, yes.'

'But we may be on the verge of proving Dad's theory!'

'Ah! I confess, in the last few hours I had forgotten your family vendetta.' He turned away from her and began to talk rapidly to Angel, apparently indifferent to the effect of his words.

Rylla's eyes stung with sudden tears. She jumped up, and walked away from the two men and looked about her as if admiring their surroundings. There was a great variety of trees, but she only recognised the palms. Some of the trees and vines were in flower despite the shortage of light. But she had no heart for photography. She felt desperately tired, jaded by the oppressive heat. And with the decline of her physical strength her morale was at very low ebb. Depression gripped her.

'Rylla?'

She kept her back towards him.

'Rylla,' he insisted, 'is something wrong?'

She turned to look at him then, and he saw the over-brilliance of her dark eyes. Her mouth trembled as she said, 'Yes.' There was a world of defeat in the monosyllable.

'Tell me.'

'It's just that I may not have my father for very much longer.' Fiercely, to stop the tears overflowing, 'But you wouldn't care a damn about that, would you?'

He took a step towards her and enfolded her in his arms.

'Rylla! Rylla! I am not *so* heartless. *Ma chère!* I am sorry! I did not think, I did not intend . . .' He took her hands in his. Warm fingers closed over hers and she made no attempt to pull away. 'I meant only to say that we have grown closer, you and I. So much so, that I had forgotten our difference of opinion.' Anxiously he studied her face. 'Tell me you believe me, that you forgive my thoughtlessness? We are friends still?'

Unable to speak, she nodded.

'*Bon!*' For a moment he held her close. 'Now let us reassure poor Angel, who must be wondering why we are so solemn.'

While the daylight lasted, they forged on. Now and then they reached a clearing, and for a while the men could sheathe their machetes. But much of the time the going was hard. Springy branches lashed back at them. Rope weed entwined itself around their ankles. Early next morning, they stumbled across an Indian village. It was only a small settlement of squat, reed-thatched houses in a riverside clearing. Jacques thought the river might be a higher stretch of the one they had forded. But here the water moved placidly, used by the women as a community laundry. For nearby lay a patchwork of colourful linens drying in the sun. It was a peaceful, idyllic scene after the trials and tribulation of their long trek.

'It is fortunate we have Angel,' Jacques said. 'These people speak an obscure dialect, unknown to me.'

'Thank goodness they're friendly,' Rylla said as they sat crosslegged to share their hosts' meal of *charqui*, a sun-dried meat accompanied by a tuberous plant similar to a potato.

'Not only friendly, but informative. They have spoken to Angel of "ancient buildings of the gods" many days' march from here.'

'Oh!' Rylla was disappointed. 'Then they're not undiscovered. There won't be anything left for us to find.'

'*Ce n'est pas necessaire*. They speak with awe of holy ground. Of the anger of the old gods. They are a very primitive people. They may have been afraid to investigate. We shall see.'

'And will we wait for Irving now?'

'*Non*. We shall not impose upon the hospitality of these people. We will barter for supplies and move on. We have blazed a trail for Irving to follow.' As Rylla continued to look doubtful, he went on, 'I give you my word, any finds will not be investigated until our party is reunited. I think perhaps you have trust in me now?'

'Yes, of course. I wasn't suggesting for a moment . . .'

'*Bon!*' His smile approved of her, and something more.

Next morning they moved on. Before long, Rylla decided the Indians might have had other reasons, besides superstition, for not exploring the terrain. At every step it became more and more water-logged. The damp encouraged thicker, more resilient undergrowth. For every fresh yard of progress they had to cross a slimy sea into which they sank knee-deep. Their only encouragement was the occasional sighting of large stones which seemed to indicate that this mire had once been crossed by a man-made causeway.

Their first real find was that of a small archway, and Rylla exclaimed with delight. Its warm stones were ablaze with a carpet of tiny yellow flowers. Then they were rewarded by the sight of quite substantial remains: grand staircases which led nowhere, the remnants of a temple, a storehouse. Revitalised by this discovery, convinced they were on the right track, Rylla got busy with her camera. But Jacques was more cautious.

'This is a very minor discovery. There is

nothing to indicate that this is any more than a subsidiary road. We may still have to turn back. But that decision we will make tomorrow,' he told Rylla, with a wry smile that appreciated her dismay. 'We can go no further tonight.'

They made camp, and Angel lit a fire. The day had been mercilessly hot and sticky, but the nights were cool. The firelight enclosed them in an intimate circle of warmth, and Rylla knew a sense of tired contentment. Even when the Indian guide had disappeared into his tent she sat on, unwilling to move and dispel the mood. She could fancy that she had sat here before in just such surroundings. Even Jacques' presence at her side felt familiar, right.

She turned to look at him, wondering what thoughts occupied his mind. But she did not need to ask as she found his eyes upon her. It was not just the firelight that gave them their glittering intensity.

'Just so must your ancestors have looked around their campfires.' Jacques tone was as fervid as his gaze. 'In you, *ma chère* Rylla, I sense an ageless, primitive femininity. But, like your hair, it is held in bondage.' He reached out and deftly freed her hair so that it tumbled about her shoulders. 'That is how you should be, *chérie*: free, untrammelled.' He lifted and examined the soft, thick tresses. Mesmerised, Rylla sat motionless. Only her dark eyes seemed alive in her beautifully modelled features. 'Rylla?' There was a questioning note in his voice, and when she did not move or answer he leant closer.

He used both hands in a tactile exploration of her hair. It was an unbelievable sensual sensation. Then he shaped the long column of her throat, the firm, strong line of her jaw.

'*Mon Dieu, que tu es belle!*' he murmured. 'Rylla, *ma chère*, I think you do not dislike me as much as your brother does?'

'I don't think I've ever disliked you.' She said it as though hypnosis drew the words from her, and he closed the gap between them.

'Ah, is it so? And you are not indifferent to me. That I know. You, too, feel this attraction that lies between us?'

'Yes.' It was useless to deny it. The quivering of her body must be as obvious to him as to herself. She longed to turn into his arms, to press herself to the length of him, to know his maleness.

'But you feel a loyalty to someone else? Is it not so?'

'Yes.' She was glad he understood.

'And you love this man—Colin, is it not?' She honestly wasn't sure any more. 'You love him with passion?' As she did not answer, he slid his hands through the curtain of her hair and cupped her head as he lowered his mouth towards hers.

A long shudder rippled through her body. Helplessly, her lips softened under his and she raised exploratory hands. His face was rough with several days growth of beard. He murmured appreciatively in his throat as her hands moved on to encircle the strong nape of his neck, caressing its muscular strength.

Gently, unalarmingly, he had manoeuvred them both so that they lay side by side. Rylla scarcely noticed the hard ground. Delicious frissons of sensation raced through her as his lips moved over her face. She did not protest when his hand slipped inside the neckline of her shirt and found the warm curves of her breasts. The heat of his hand was searing through the flimsy material of her bra. Her nipples tightened, ached. His tongue probed her mouth deeper and deeper, his intensity generating an answering heat within her.

She slid her hands beneath the coarse material of his shirt, her palms flat against the silky smooth chest hair. Jacques muttered something under his breath, and impatient fingers unfastened her shirt. His mouth was warm in the deep cleft between her breasts, trailing a path from one taut peak to another.

But his hands became more demanding, probing the waist band of her jeans. She felt his sudden shudder of pure sexual hunger and knew this had to stop. She tried to pull away.

'Non, ma chère! Stay! Ah, Rylla, ma belle, how I want you.' His voice was thick, passion-filled, more strongly accented than usual.

'No, Jacques! No!' She knew she sounded panicky, and she was afraid. She was afraid he would refuse to stop, that he might not be able to stop now.

'No?' His mouth, still at her breast, was exquisite torture. 'Are you sure, *ma chère*?'

'Quite sure.' But as he lifted his head she almost cried out again, with a sensation of loss. However, returning sanity had cooled the raging fever that had possessed her. 'This isn't love.'

'No? But to love is to hunger for the beloved? Is it not so?'

She shook her head, but not in denial of his words. He was physically attracted to her. They'd been drawn together by circumstances into an unusual intimacy. But he hadn't said that he loved her, only that he wanted her. The trouble was, Rylla suspected her feelings went deeper than that.

He released her and sat up and she felt him shrug.

'So be it. It is, after all, scarcely the time or the place.'

CHAPTER SIX

WHEN Rylla woke next morning she couldn't think for a moment what was worrying her. Then she remembered. Today they might have to retrace their long, arduous route through the jungle. But it wasn't just that. She suspected she was falling in love with Jacques Fresnay, and she wasn't sure that love meant the same to him as it did to her.

One thing she did know. Whatever the outcome of her feelings for Jacques, she wasn't, had never been in love with Colin Philby. If she had been, it would have formed a shield and defence against all other attractions. At the first opportunity she must write to Colin, ending their relationship. That was only fair.

The going that day was heavier than ever. For hour after hour the men hacked their way through a plantation of *sachapelma*, giant tubers that resembled rhubarb. The colour of the enormous swollen leaves merged depressingly from black to deep purple. The machetes could clear only a few feet in what seemed as many hours. The air was humid, the flies busy. All Rylla's energies were concentrated just on putting one foot before another.

'*Mon Dieu!* Look at that!'

142

At first, Rylla thought it was a mirage. They had emerged from the plantation and ahead of them rose a mountainside. But what a mountainside! Its jungle-infested foothills were a series of narrow steps, unmistakably Inca terraces.

'Somewhere up there may be our city,' Jacques said.

'You think it will still be there?'

'If it ever existed, something will be there. Inca cities do not vanish easily, *ma chère*. They were built to endure even earthquakes. See how nature bars the way to any would-be invader.' He pointed to the deep narrow canyon that lay between them and their goal. An unpleasant miasma steamed up from the depths and insects hovered about their heads.

'Judging by the steps, the whole thing must be enormous! Almost the size of Machu Picchu?'

'And impossible that just we few should investigate it,' Jacques said.

'But when Irving catches us up . . .'

'Even then, *ma chère*, we will be too few. So colossal a site will need many workers, many years of study.'

Rylla was incredulous. 'You mean, we've come all this way and then we're not going to do anything about it?'

'Calm down!' He laughed at her dismay. 'Naturally, we shall make preliminary assessments. But then we must return with a team. We must make the site accessible by air. The jungle must be cleared, a helicopter landing-site constructed. Stores and equipment must be flown in. These things take time and organisation.'

'Of course!' Rylla exclaimed. 'I'm as bad as Andy. I had visions of us digging for Inca gold and going home with fantastic stories to tell.'

'If our city exists, we shall have stories to tell, *ma chère*, never fear. But, as they say, "first reach your city". We have to bridge that gorge.'

In the last few days Rylla had been awed by the strength and stamina Jacques had shown throughout all the ordeals they'd faced. Officially, Angel was their guide, but over difficult terrain it had always been Jacques who led the way. Yet surely even he couldn't overcome this obstacle?

Next day, the rest of their party came up with them.

'Our track petered out. But all we had to do was follow your "trail of destruction",' Andy told Rylla. 'Bit of a strong-arm man, your Professor Fresnay, isn't he?'

'Yes, he is!' Andy's tone had been sarcastic. Rylla spoke in earnest, defensively. It didn't pass unnoticed.

'Getting a bit partisan, aren't you, Sis? You haven't forgotten who he is? The aged "P"s *bête noire*? What about the family feud?'

'As far as I'm concerned, there is no feud. Dad's quarrel with Jacques is professional, not personal. If he knew Jacques . . .'

'As you obviously think you do? Still fancy him, don't you?'

'It's not just that.' Rylla didn't waste time denying it. Her brother knew her too well. 'He's thoughtful, considerate and brave. He saved my life, Andy.'

'Well, I suppose that might put him back in Dad's good books. You always were his favourite. But does this mean you've gone completely over to the opposition? That you're supporting Jacques' theory about Huascar, and not Dad's?'

'No. Not exactly. I want to see Dad proved right, of course I do. But if he is wrong I'd as soon it was Jacques discovered it than anyone else. He's not the sort to gloat or make capital out of it.'

'Quite a love affair, it seems!'

'No!' Her tone was sharp. 'Jacques and I are friends, colleagues. Nothing more.'

'"The lady doth protest too much, methinks"!'

'I mean it, Andy. And don't you dare say anything like that to anyone else.'

'Well, I think Jeni was hoping it'd develop into something more than that.'

'Jeni?'

'Haven't you noticed? Poor old Jeni is head over heels in love with Irving. He hasn't noticed it either. With you out of the running, he might. But you stick to your guns, by all means. Irving's a rich prize, and I'd just as soon you won.'

'Don't be silly, Andy,' Rylla said automatically. Her mind was still on the amazing news. It accounted for a lot she hadn't understood. She had become accustomed to thinking of Irving as her friend. But she had never wanted to marry him. And Jeni couldn't know that. She resolved that somehow, tactfully, she would let the other girl know exactly how things stood.

Irving was anxious to solve the problem of bridging the gorge.

'Once, there would have been a suspension bridge, made of *liana* rope. The best thing we can hope for is to find a tree we can fell. One tall enough to span the width as it falls. I suggest you girls stay here. Jeni, could you rustle up a meal if Angel lights a fire? Rylla, this might be a good opportunity for you to take some photographs?'

'Yes, thanks.'

Rylla had already spotted several extravagantly colourful flowers growing just at the edge of the jungle. Orchids, she suspected. Blue, purple, red and yellow. It was no use picking specimens. But she could make a photographic record of blooms which were more exotic than any she'd ever seen in a florist's selection. She was soon happily engrossed taking shot after shot, heedless of the occasional spine that penetrated the soft skin of her fingers.

A little further ahead she saw other flowers which looked like lilies. She pushed through a tangle of *lianas* to reach them. With growing excitement she found more and more wondrous species.

She did not realise just how far she'd wandered until she realised she could no longer hear the river rushing through the gorge. Still, all she had to do was to retrace her steps from one species of flower to another.

But the jungle seemed to be getting more dense, shrouded in forbidding darkness. She must have taken a wrong direction. There must have been more than one clump of those gigantic lilies. Don't panic, she told herself. But it was eerily still here. There was an unnatural silence which emphasised the sound of an insistent inner voice that whispered, 'lost, lost, lost'.

Once she stopped, rooted to the spot, heart pounding, as she mistook a snake-like *liana* for the real thing.

Again she plunged forward into the wilderness. Her approach sent up a flight of small brightly hued birds which in turn disturbed a colony of monkeys. The small creatures leapt from tree to tree, scolding vociferously.

'Oh, shut up! You can have your rotten jungle, as far as I'm concerned,' she joked. But her voice sounded small and feeble, and she wished she hadn't spoken aloud. Perhaps, instead of blundering on and getting more and more lost, it would be sensible to stay put and call for help. The others would hear her. She couldn't be that far away from them.

'Hello! Andy? Irving? Jacques?' she was shouting now. But her voice sounded thin and quavery, muffled by the thick foliage around her.

There was no answering cry. She tried again. Nothing. She could have sworn that the trees were closing in on her, as if to deprive her of light and air. Nonsense, she told herself. It was getting late and darkness fell quickly in the jungle. She must hurry.

She tripped over the skeletal roots of a tree and fell heavily. Winded, she lay still for a moment, hoping she hadn't twisted her ankle again. She scrambled up, began to run, pushing her way through the undergrowth, heedless of the scratches of thorny branches. Her greatest fear now it was growing dark was that she might encounter a real snake hanging from a tree. There were many varieties of poisonous snakes in South America.

Fatigue slowed her progress. Her body ached with weariness. She was tortured by the ever-present flies. Her clothes were ripped in several places. Then, as she'd known it would, darkness fell, making it impossible to go any further.

She pressed her back against the bole of a tree and slid to the ground. She sat hunched up, arms folded about her knees. Fear was a hot, dry taste in her mouth. She was truly alone in a wilderness of silence. But she fought against despair. She mustn't allow herself to believe this was the end, death from some predator or from exposure.

The monkeys began their usual evening chatter. Vines, twisted about the giant trees, rustled drily, sinisterly. Her fingers were sore where the spines of the deceptively lovely flowers had wounded her.

She must have dozed for a while. For she had no

idea how long she'd been sitting there when she saw a gleam of light through the trees. It was a fugitive glimmer at first, then a steady beam that darted here and there. Torchlight! At first, she couldn't believe it. It was wishful thinking. Then she heard someone call her name. Only one person said her name in that way.

'Jacques!' She got to her feet. All pain and discomfort was forgotten. Strength flowed back into her at the knowledge of his presence. 'Over here!' She stumbled towards him.

'Rylla! *Quelle bêtise!*' He sounded furiously angry. 'To wander off alone!' His hands made a swift exploration of her body before coming to rest on her shoulders. 'Are you hurt?'

'Only a bit scratched. I didn't mean to go so far,' she said tremulously. At his touch, it was not only relief that weakened her sinews.

'One never does. But the jungle is a siren. It draws one on with promises of new delights around every corner.'

'Yes,' she agreed ruefully. 'That's just what it did.'

'Have you any idea of what might have happened to you?' He still sounded angry.

'Only too well.' She shuddered and his grasp tightened, drawing her closer. 'I'm very relieved you found me so soon. Thank you.'

'I would have searched all night if necessary, Rylla *ma chère!*' His tone was milder. Instead of gripping her shoulders, his hands gently massaged tense muscles.

'I can't think why!' she joked unsteadily.

'Can you not, *chèrie*?' He held her tightly. 'Then perhaps it is time I . . .'

'Shouldn't we be getting back?' she asked hastily. 'The others will be worrying.'

'*Non!*' But his hands dropped to his side. 'We move no further tonight. It would be foolhardy. We stay here until first light.'

'But there's no shelter, no protection.'

'More than if I had not discovered you. Now, at least, you have a sleeping-bag.' He pulled a rolled-up bundle from his knapsack. 'And you have me,' she could hear the smile in his voice, 'to protect you from the snakes.'

But who would protect her from *him*?

'I'm not sharing your sleeping-bag again,' she told him, and heard him chuckle.

'It would be more polite, *chèrie*, to wait until you are invited. As it is, you need have no fear. For there are two. Mine and yours.'

'Oh!' She felt extremely foolish and—yes, a little disappointed.

'But first you must be hungry? I have some *chocolat* and a flask of soup Jeni prepared before I left camp.'

'Did you find a way across the canyon?' she asked when she'd finished eating.

'*Mais oui*. There is a tree which will serve. Tomorrow we will chop it down.'

'Oh, good.' There was silence again. An unnatural silence. She had not imagined the tension, or his reaction to it.

'Rylla!' She started at the touch of his hand on her arm. 'I have been wishing to speak with you. We are alone now and there is plenty of time. There will be no interruptions.'

She jumped up. There was no need to pretend to shiver.

'It's getting cold, isn't it? I think I'll get into my sleeping-bag.'

He rose, too. He took her by the upper arms in a firm grasp.

'Listen to me, *ma chère*. You cannot always be running away from the truth. There is nothing to fear.'

'The truth?' Her emotions were already confused. Perhaps her judgement was, too. 'I don't know what you ...'

'Yes, you do,' he contradicted gently. His nearness was drugging her senses. 'I wish to speak to you of love.' And, as she caught her breath, 'No, hear me out. When we first met, I recognised the instant attraction between us. But you have fought against it. At first, I thought it was because of my disagreement with your father. Then I thought perhaps you and Irving ...'

'I'm very fond of Irving,' she put in hastily.

'Fond?' he said scornfully. 'That is how one speaks of a brother, of an uncle, *n'est-ce pas*? Me, I have watched you and Irving together. There is not this flame between you, that we feel, you and I. And when we found you missing, his concern was for the daughter of an old friend, not for the woman he loved.'

'The physical attraction we feel——' she began.

'Is not love? So you have told me. But without it, *ma chère*, there is no love either. You could not love someone you find physically repulsive?' His right hand moved up to her neck, and his finger traced the line of her jaw. He kissed her softly.

'No, but . . .'

'Then, may not attraction be the beginning of love?' In the pitch blackness she couldn't see him, but she could feel his warm breath on her face. 'Can you deny that more than liking has grown between us, *ma chère*?'

She stirred faintly, uneasily in his clasp, as she imagined how he would be in the act of love.

'No, but . . .'

'So why cannot you accept that this is love? Why not let me show you my love is nothing to fear? Love is to be gloried in, welcomed.' Both his arms were around her, his fingers caressing her spine an insidiously seductive motion.

'I know that,' she murmured weakly. 'But there's Colin. I haven't . . .'

'Colin! Bah!' Emphatically, 'For you, he is the wrong man.'

'You can't *know* that. You've never met him. You've never seen us together.'

'I *do* know, because I know *I* am the man for you. And you know it too, Rylla, only you won't admit it. I have known it from the first moment I saw you. I have watched you,' his voice grew husky, '*mon dieu*, how I have watched you! In your unguarded moments I have seen the soul of you.'

He took one of her hands and held it against his broad chest. 'Feel how my heart beats for you.' She wanted him to go on. There was seduction in his tone of voice. But was there sincerity, too? 'I love you, Rylla. *Je t'aime toujours, de tout mon coeur!* For me, you are of more value than the greatest horde of Inca gold. When I thought you were lost, it was not Irving, but I who . . .'

'Jacques, please! Don't!' She turned her head from side to side, avoiding the warm compulsion of his mouth. 'I'd like to believe you, but . . .'

'Then half the battle is won!' He was exultant. 'I am right. You *do* care for me.'

'I'd like to believe you,' she repeated firmly, 'but I can't be certain you're not saying all these things just to get me to . . .'

'And I thought you had learned to trust me,' he reproached her. 'But, if that is all you fear, let me tell you this. If you will permit me to hold you for a while, to kiss and caress you a little, I will be content. It will be difficult. I am only human. But until we return to civilisation that is all I will ask of you. But once we are married! *Eh bien!*'

'Married?' she said faintly.

'Yes, of course!' He sounded surprised. '*Will* you marry me, Rylla?'

'Oh, Jacques!' She was half laughing, half crying, and she said his name on a wave of longing. 'Do you really mean it? Because if you do . . .'

'*Mais oui!* Of course I mean it, little fool,' he said tenderly. 'But I warn you,' with mock fierceness, 'once you *are* mine, I shall be a demanding, tireless lover. Shall you weary of my attentions, do you think?'

There was laughter in his voice, but she answered him seriously, sincerely. 'Oh, no! It would be wonderful to be loved like that.'

'Then, *ma chère*,' he said huskily, 'all you have to do is to love and be loved. You have only to say the right words.'

'The words?'

'*Je t'aime*,' he prompted softly. 'Let me hear you say it in my own tongue. But I forgot. You do not yet love me. Perhaps I love too much, too soon? Will you let me teach you to love me, *chèrie*? I promise you I will be a patient tutor.'

'There's no need,' she told him on a long soft sigh. '*Je t'aime*, Jacques! I *do* love you. I think I've known it for some time.'

'And you will marry me?'

'Yes. Jacques?' Courage welled within her. 'And if you want me . . .'

'*If* I want you?' he said throatily.

'If you want me, there's no need to wait.' Somehow it was easier to say it under the cover of primeval darkness, but even so she felt her cheeks flood with warmth at her own daring.

'You want me, *ma chère*? Now?'

'Yes.' She whispered the words so softly that he had to bend his head. 'Are you shocked?' As her lips brushed the lobe of his ear she felt his body harden.

'Shocked? How should I be shocked?
Heart of my heart!'

They *had* shared a sleeping-bag, after all. During
the night she woke only once, to be reassured
immediately by Jacques' nearness, the sound of his
steady breathing, the knowledge of his love for
her.

With the daylight Rylla woke to a sense of
incredulous happiness. She loved and was loved.
Briefly, there had been pain. But he had been
gentle with her, considerate of her inexperience,
yet there had been no holding back. No expression, no gesture of love had been too extravagant
as he led her towards the final fulfilment, until at
last their passion had mounted, soared, climaxed
together. Their demands of each other had been
total, as primitive and unbounded as the wild
luxuriance of their surroundings.

'Of what are you thinking, *ma chère?*'

Jacques' eyes were open. All their bright blue
attention was focused on the strong lines of her
face, from which his loving had erased all reserve.
The look she turned on him was meltingly tender.

'That today is the first day of the rest of my
life—of our life,' she told him huskily.

It was impossible to move any closer to him.
They were already intimately entwined. But
Rylla attempted it.

'Witch!' he murmured.

Her breasts were crushed against the hard wall
of his chest, her hips one with his. Her eagerly

parted lips were softly sensuous. She delighted in
the feel of his skin under her fingers, his warm,
musky scent, his hard muscularity. Tremors of
reaction coursed through her as she stroked and
caressed.

'What are you trying to do to me?' Jacques
murmured as she arched towards him, offering the
soft incitement of her body.

'I should have thought that was obvious,' she
teased between soft kisses.

'Yes,' he said wryly. '*Mais non!* Rylla, *ma chère.*'
His voice was throaty. He was undeniably
aroused. Yet he sounded amused. 'Would that we
could make love all day. But we must return to the
others. There is work to be done.' With a final
hard kiss upon her moistened lips he put her
firmly from him.

'Jacques!' she protested.

'Later, *chérie,*' he told her tenderly. 'Remember,
we have the rest of our lives.'

'Rylla, love! Thank God, you're safe!' The others
gathered round as Irving greeted her with one of
his prolonged bearhugs. But he scolded her, too.
'That was a damn fool trick, wandering off like
that. How could I have faced Matt if anything had
happened to you?'

Jacques was right, she thought. Irving's affection for her was just that. She was glad. She would
have hated him to be hurt. There was Colin to be
told, of course. But somehow she didn't think he
would suffer too much. Gloria Ray was more his

type. She would fit in better with the life-style he wanted for himself.

The felled tree made a breathtakingly narrow tightrope across the gorge and its seething current. Rylla shuddered, conscious of the gaping maw beneath her. Even with Jacques' hand to steady her she couldn't forget the jagged rocks creamed by racing waters. It only needed one false step. But at last they were all safely on the other side.

Even with this obstacle behind them, their assault upon the mountain fortress was not easy. The lower, man-made terraces were densely overgrown with vine and creeper. Even when they reached a wide flight of stone steps every one had to be individually cleared.

Jacques and Rylla reached the summit ahead of the others. Jeni seemed to be having difficulty with her breathing again.

'This would have been the city plaza,' Jacques told Rylla.

It was difficult, she thought with a fugitive glance at him, to see in Jacques the fervid lover of last night. Today he seemed totally divorced from all emotion. He was treating her as though she were just another expedition member to be guided to safety. He had given as much care to Jeni as to her. If only he would smile at her, she thought longingly, with the expression in his eyes only she could interpret. A quotation she'd heard somewhere ran through her mind a repetitive refrain: 'Man's love is of man's life a thing apart, 'Tis woman's whole existence.' Whatever she was doing, she thought, she could never be unaware of Jacques, of her love for him.

The summit was overgrown too, but beyond it they could see the massive walls of other buildings, wreathed in clinging growth. No wonder the city had remained undiscovered so long. Not even the keenest aerial camera would have penetrated the dense greenery.

'The Temple of the Sun!' Rylla would have recognised the pyramid shape even without her visit to Machu Picchu. Along its walls, trapezoidal niches held figures that Rylla realised incredulously were made of gold.

'I think we can safely assume we are the only white people ever to set foot here,' Jacques told her. 'No one was allowed to own gold except the supreme Inca. And no Spaniard would have left these treasures untouched.'

'Pity those statues are too heavy for us to carry,' Andy said regretfully.

'We touch nothing, *mon ami*,' Jacques told him pleasantly but firmly. 'All will go to the museums.'

'I know how Andy feels, though,' Rylla said. 'It would be nice to have a souvenir, just to prove we were really here.' She would have gone forward to investigate the temple, but Jacques restrained her.

'Wait!' He moved ahead, his machete probing the undergrowth. Something moved, something long, black and sinuous, and Rylla screamed. However foolish it made her seem, she just couldn't help it. But Jacques' reaction were lightning-swift. His machete came down just behind the evil head.

'A *jararaca*!' Irving exclaimed. 'One of the most aggressive and poisonous snakes in existence.'

And she might have walked blindly into its path. Rylla shuddered. Once again Jacques had saved her. Tremulously, she thanked him.

To her relief, there were no more snakes. Once the gigantic vines had been hacked away from the rectangular doorway, the building was found to be dry and free from pests. But as the men passed their flashlights over the interior, Rylla shuddered for another reason.

The light revealed strange carvings, a sinister, concave altar stone. She felt her mouth go dry with awe. Perhaps they were the first people to stand here since those worshippers of long ago, who'd thought nothing of human sacrifice.

'There are no such things as ghosts, *ma chère*,' Jacques said when she voiced her thoughts.

'I'm not so sure.' Beyond the light of the torches she was conscious of shadows which might conceal the shades of long-dead priests who had served the sun god.

'We'll make this our base,' Irving decided. 'It'll be an ideal place to sleep and eat.'

But no one was ready for food and rest. They were all anxious to explore. Outside the building, an open stairway led to the truncated top of the temple. At the summit stood the sun-catcher, or sundial. It was almost identical to that at Machu

Picchu, except that the central *stele* was made of solid gold.

From the temple roof they had a view over the whole of the city and the jungle beyond. Irving suggested Rylla should take a shot of the way the streets ran out from the plaza, crossing each other in a grill pattern.

This done, they descended the staircase to investigate the large stone structures standing some distance to the rear of the temple. At first, Rylla thought they were *oubliettes* for the sun god's sacrificial victims. But Irving said they would have been used for the storage of corn, maize and other foodstuffs. There were traces still of their original contents. Jacques thrust an exploratory hand into a dusty greyish substance, which at first appeared to be common earth.

'Powdered potato!' he exclaimed.

'*Potato?*' Rylla said incredulously.

'Potato,' he confirmed. 'Dried potato isn't a twentieth-century invention. The Indians powdered it to preserve it. It was a long process. They had to freeze it, crush it and freeze it again. But dried like that, they lasted for ever.'

'I wouldn't like to eat any of it,' was Andy's predictable comment.

'But it's not just potato.' Irving discovered. His tone was all the more even because of the tremendous excitement that gripped him. 'Look here!'

'*Mon Dieu!*'

'Wealth beyond the dreams of avarice!' This was Andy.

'Atahualpa's treasure!'

Hidden below the powdered potato in the first stone bin were beautifully decorated drinking-cups and bowls. There were belts, brooches, small gold items modelled in the form of toads, alligators, insects and cats. Rylla seized one of these objects. The gold had been painted black except for the collar. The face of the beast was half-human, the menacing teeth longer than any species of cat known to man.

'That's not by the Incas!' Jacques took it from her and examined it carefully. 'It was the Chavin tribe who worshipped a cat god.'

'How did it get here?' Her fingers itched to take it back. It was the most fascinating thing she'd ever seen.

'Quite easily, I imagine. The Incas conquered race after race. They moved whole tribes from one place to another and forced the Quechuan language on them. They did not care what gods were worshipped, so long as the conquered race acknowledged the supremacy of the sun. One of their slaves was probably Chavin, and brought his pet god with him. Just this one item is of tremendous value,' he mused. 'As to the whole of the treasure! Inestimable!'

'We can't do any more tonight,' Irving decided. 'It's nearly dark. Tomorrow we'll start cataloguing this stuff and see what else there is.'

Over their evening meal and far into the night

they talked over their amazing finds. The two girls had sleeping-bags at one side of the temple, the men at the other. Rylla thought yearningly of the previous night, when she and Jacques had shared a sleeping-bag. She wondered if he was remembering, if he was wanting her. She stirred restlessly, unable to sleep, taut with the longing to touch him, to be touched.

As always, the sleepless small hours brought worries. Her hands were still throbbing with scratches. She wondered how her father would take the news of her love for Jacques, his professional rival. The last thing she wanted to do in Matthew's state of health was to precipitate an angry scene.

But at last she slept, though her dreams were filled with wraith-like priests, with human sacrifice, with vindictive gods with cat-like faces. And when she woke, it was with the thought that she did not after all care much for the little idol.

Next morning they extended their searches. Rylla, though feeling tired and heavy-eyed, arranged their finds in suitable groups to be photographed.

'A penny for your thoughts, *ma chère*?'

She sat back on her heels and looked up at him a little shyly.

'I was thinking about Dad. Jacques, I'm afraid he's not going to be pleased about us.'

'I see!' His tone was grave, his blue eyes intent on her lovely troubled face. 'His opinion weighs heavily with you, is it not so?'

'It always has,' she began, a troubled frown wrinkling her smooth brow, 'but . . .'

'And your brother?'

'Jacques! Rylla! Take a look at this!' Irving's excited exclamation interrupted their tête-à-tête. Helped by Andy, he was struggling to remove something from one of the larger storage bins.

By the time Rylla scrambled up Jacques was already leaning over Irving's shoulder.

'*Mon Dieu!* It is! It must be! The chain of Huayna Cápac!'

'Who's he when he's at home?' Andy demanded. Then, incredulously, 'Is this thing real gold? *All* of it?'

'It most certainly is.'

'Why on earth would anyone want a chain that size?' Rylla asked.

'Huayna Cápac was father to Atahualpa and Huascar. Atahualpa was a bastard. Huascar was the rightful son and, when he came of age, like all young men he had to go through a ceremony known as the Festival of the Trial of Manhood. Part of this ceremony was a ritual dance. For ordinary men the dancers would have carried a chain of black, white, red and yellow wool. But for his son's ceremony Huayna Cápac ordered a great chain of gold to be made, long enough to go twice around the main square of Cuzco. It was as thick as a man's arm and took many men to carry it. And that,' Jacques concluded, 'is what we have here. It is also proof of my theory. The treasure here at Huacaintiraymi *is* that of Huascar, not

Atahualpa.' It was quietly said, and without triumph. But his eyes were on Rylla's face.

'I see,' she said quietly. There might have been no one there but the two of them. 'Then Dad was wrong, after all. He'll be very disappointed.'

Proved right, Matthew might have accepted the news that she intended to marry Jacques Fresnay. But now?

'I am sorry, *ma chère*, truly sorry.' Jacques set a hand on her shoulder, but for once she didn't react. 'History cannot be changed to suit the needs of one man. Is it not so?'

'True,' she said dispiritedly. 'But how can I tell him about us now?'

'Perhaps you would prefer it to remain our secret a little longer?'

'Yes.' Perhaps once Matthew had got over his initial chagrin . . . 'You don't mind?'

'Oh, I mind, *chérie*! But I can be patient when necessary.'

'Rylla,' Irving called a little testily. 'We need some shots of this chain before we cover it up again. There's no way we can move it.'

They spent two more days seeking out and cataloguing the inexhaustible treasures. As well as precious stones and gold, there was pottery of an almost metallic hardness. Its crude colouring had survived the years. In one of the buildings they discovered a painted fresco of a triumphal procession. It showed the supreme Inca being carried on a litter, followed by musicians playing drums and tambourines, bells and rattles. Flutes and trumpets made from seashells formed the core of the wind instruments.

Though she had not admitted it to anyone, Rylla was feeling far from well. Her head throbbed continually, and her body ached. She dared not tell anyone. Sickness had no place on an expedition such as this.

Afraid she might run out of film before her task was completed, she checked the various compartments of her camera case, hoping to find unused film. Instead, she came across Matthew's forgotten letter. She sat back on her heels and brushed droplets of sweat from her eyes. She really did feel most peculiar.

'Dearest Rylla,' she read, 'You know now why I'm not with you. But don't worry about my health, because I intend to be around for a long time yet. You'll also know that Irving is roping in the Frenchman instead. I suppose I should mind, but being ill has rather altered my priorities. I find I'm more concerned with storing up treasures in the next world than search for them in this. Atahualpa's treasure? Huascar's treasure? What the heck does it matter? I hate to admit it, but Fresnay's the logical person to take my place. His knowledge of Peru is phenomenal for one so young. Still, he's had an advantage I lacked at his age, money.' But Jacques had denied being wealthy. Rylla turned the page, noting as she did so her hands were trembling. 'But then I married for love, not money. Having a rich wife has furthered his career.'

Jacques was *married*! Rylla rubbed her aching eyes and read her father's letter over and over again, but there was no misunderstanding it. Jacques had lied to her. He wasn't free to marry anyone.

How naïve she'd been to suppose he'd wanted to make love to her because he'd fallen for her. They'd wanted each other, and the inevitable had happened. *His* love had been an illusion. A physical need satisfied, that was all. Slowly she stood up. Inside she was numb and hurting, and she wanted to hurt back. She would find Jacques and confront him with this letter. But as she took the first step she felt nausea rise in her throat, before a rushing, roaring sound, as of a giant waterfall, drowned her in merciful oblivion.

CHAPTER SEVEN

'THAT's it, Miss Quarmby. Easy now! Everything's going to be all right. No, don't try to talk. You've been very ill. But you're going to be fine.'

From the nightmarish world of ancient priests, of human sacrifice, of the evil grimacing cat god, there was a sensation of travelling back through a long, dark tunnel towards light. Rylla emerged into a shifting blur of white. There were voices that sounded like a record played at the wrong speed, slurred and incomprehensible. Headache. A vile taste in the mouth. But, above all, dread. Dread of returning consciousness, of remembering what it was that lay so heavily upon her heart.

'Lift her head, nurse. Get her to sip this, if she can.'

Blissfully cool hands on her head. Firm fingers on her pulse. The moisture spilling over dry, clumsy lips and trickling down her chin.

'Her temperature's coming down. It's almost normal. Let her sleep now. Next time she wakes up she should be coherent.'

Yes, Rylla thought hazily. Let her sleep. Let her go on sleeping. Never wake up. Don't want to wake up. To wake up was to have total recall. Recall meant unhappiness.

* * *

'Good! You're back in the land of the living! Now we can have a little chat.'

An olive-skinned nurse in a crisp white uniform sat on the side of the bed.

'I'm in hospital?' Rylla discovered wonderingly, as she looked around her. Her last conscious memory was of intense heat, of a dreadful feeling of malaise, of forcing herself to photograph hundreds of precious objects, because whatever happened she mustn't let the others down. And then ... 'don't remember' something inside her screamed. 'How did I get here?'

'I understand you were carried some of the way. By the men of your expedition. When they reached civilisation they were able to telephone for a helicopter to pick you up.'

'Where is this?'

'You're in Lima.'

'And my friends?'

'They took it in turns to stay by your bedside until we could assure them you were out of danger. Then, I understand, the men went back into the interior. You had just made an important find, is that right?'

'Yes.' But the nurse was referring to their discovery of Huacaintiraymi. Rylla was thinking of Matthew's letter. It was no use trying not to remember. Its contents were engraved, not just upon her mind, but upon her heart. Jacques had lied to her. Jacques was married. She sat up straight in bed and asked urgently, 'How soon can I get out of here?'

'Oh, come now!' The nurse was encouraging. 'You've been very ill. You'll be as weak as a kitten for a long time.'

'What's been wrong with me?'

'A fever, brought on by the infection in your hands.' For the first time, Rylla looked down at herself. Her hands were heavily swathed in bandages. 'Your friends think you must have been scratched by a thorned flower peculiar to the area you were in, and you were suffering from septicaemia, blood poisoning.'

'And just that made me feel so ill?'

'Ye—es,' the nurse sounded hesitant. 'Miss Quarmby, did you have any idea that you were expecting a baby?'

For a moment, Rylla could not speak. Then, 'A baby?' She squeaked the words. She sank back on the pillows. 'Oh, my God! Pregnant!'

'Yes, we discovered that among the many routine tests carried out on you. It's very early days yet, of course, but unmistakable.'

'How long have I been here?'

'Three weeks, nearly four.'

'Does—does anyone else know about this?'

'No. As you didn't appear to be married or engaged, we decided it was best to wait until you could be told yourself. It could have caused embarrassment to tell your friends.'

It certainly could, Rylla thought. Thank God

Jacques didn't know!

'And I don't want any of them to be told,' she stated to the nurse. 'Is that clear?'

'Quite clear, my dear. Of course, you'll want to tell the father yourself. One of those two gentlemen *is* the father?'

Rylla didn't confirm or deny it. The less anyone knew the better.

'I'd like to see the doctor,' she said. 'I want to know exactly how soon I can get out of here. I have to go back to England. It's very important.'

'My dear, for your own sake, for the sake of the child, don't be in too much of a hurry. Blood poisoning makes you weak. You need to recuperate.'

'When did Ja ... When did the men go back into the interior?'

'The day before yesterday. That was the first moment we could be sure you were out of danger.'

'How long have they gone for?'

'I've no idea. Perhaps Miss Grayson will be able to help you?'

'Jeni's still here?'

'Yes. She felt you would want one familiar face around when you were feeling better. She's gone back to her hotel to rest, but she'll be here again at visiting time. Now we'll see about a light meal for you, and then you must get some sleep. Sleep is a great healer.'

It might be, for illness. But no amount of sleep could cure what ailed her. If Rylla had been stunned when she read Matt's letter, now she was appalled. Pregnant. After only one occasion. She'd known it was possible, of course. But you always thought it couldn't happen to you. Besides it hadn't mattered then. Not when she'd thought Jacques was going to marry her.

And now she'd never know his lovemaking again. She closed her eyes tightly, but the tears managed to force their way under her lids. She wanted to go home. The challenge of exploring unknown places had lost all its appeal. She wanted to go home, where flowers didn't spike the unwary with poison that seeped beneath the skin. She wanted to go home, where she need never see Jacques Fresnay again.

'Rylla, thank goodness you're better! You had us really worried.' Promptly at visiting time, Jeni appeared. 'I'm afraid I haven't brought you anything. I wasn't sure what you could have. How are you feeling?'

'Fed up!' Rylla told her. 'All I want to do is get out of here and go home. But I'm told I'm not fit enough.'

'You know Irving's taken a team of men back to Huacaintiraymi? He's registered his find with the authorities, and now he's mad keen to get a helicopter landing-strip organised.

'And Jacques?' She had to ask.

'I think he's gone home for a few days, to France. But he and Irving left you all sorts of good wishes. I'm staying on in Lima while you're still in hospital.'

'That's very sweet of you. But that won't be for long, if I have my way.'

And the next time Jeni visited, Rylla told her, 'I'm going home the day after tomorrow. I've signed my discharge. My flight's booked and I've wired my father to expect me.'

'What will you do when you've seen your father?' Jeni asked.

'Convalesce for a bit, I suppose. I'm not entirely stupid, though the staff here seem to think so. Then I'll get all the films developed and printed. That will take quite a while. And, providing Dad's OK, I'll take another assignment, I suppose.' She tried to force enthusiasm into her voice. Very soon, she wouldn't be up to any hectic overseas trips. But if she were to keep her secret she must act normally.

'Another assignment? With Irving?'

'Good lord, no!' Rylla remembered some unfinished business. 'Jeni, I don't want you to think I'm prying, but there was something Andy said. I want you to know there's nothing between me and Irving, that there never has been.'

Jeni did not deny her interest.

'But he's always spoken so glowingly of you,' she said doubtfully. 'He seems very fond of you.'

'He is. At least, I hope he is, but only as a friend, and because I'm my father's daughter. I take it

Andy was right? I wish you luck, Jeni, and every happiness.'

The Customs official checked Rylla's passport.

'And now if you'll just open your cases, *señorita*?'

'Of course!' Rylla hoisted her few belongings on to the counter top. There wasn't much, just a small suitcase, an overnight bag and the large case containing all her camera equipment. She was unconcerned about the routine check. So what followed was an unpleasant shock.

'Have you any explanation for this, *señorita*?' His search had uncovered something which certainly had no business in her camera case. It lay there, staring malevolently up at her. The jewelled eyes sparkled. The gold collar gleamed. The fangs were bared in a mocking grimace as they had in her nightmares. Never had it looked so evil.

'The cat god!' she gasped.

'Quite possibly, *señorita*!' The official's tone was dry. 'Whatever it is, can you explain how it came to be in your possession?'

'I've just been on an expedition into the interior, with Professor Wilder. But I don't know . . .' Rylla stopped. She'd been about to say she had no idea how the Chavin cat god had got into her camera case. But a dreadful possibility had just occurred to her.

'I see!' Never had two words been fraught with such threatening emphasis. 'In that case, I must ask you to come with me. I am very much afraid, *señorita*, that you will not be taking your flight today—or, indeed, any flight for some time to come.'

Rylla was left to cool her heels, guarded by a stern-looking woman who spoke no English. She had plenty of time to think about her suspicion of how the golden idol came to be in her belongings. There was only the one very unpleasant conclusion: Andy must have put it there. Her brother was always dissatisfied with his own financial state. Throughout their trip, he'd spoken longingly of discovering treasure. She remembered the expression on his face when they'd discovered Huascar's horde. She remembered what Jacques had said in Andy's hearing, 'Just this one item is of tremendous value.'

But what a stupid, irresponsible thing her brother had done! She acquitted him of deliberate malice. Obviously, it hadn't occurred to him that Customs would search her camera equipment. Had he even considered the effect it might have on their father if she were arrested? And, apart from that, he'd put her in a very invidious position. Not only with the Peruvian authorities, but with Irving. And Jacques? He'd be bound to remember her wistful comment about souvenirs.

It was unlikely she'd be believed if she said the item had been planted on her. But she couldn't involve Andy. There was just an outside chance she was wrong. And if she was right? Their situation would be reversed. He would be occupying this cell, a situation which might equally well cause Matthew Quarmby to have a relapse. And Andy would lose his job. Irving was scrupulously honest about any finds. This might be the most priceless horde ever to come his way, but the older man would never succumb to temptation. And he would expect his colleagues to be as above reproach.

Of more immediate concern, however, what was going to happen to *her*?

Half an hour later, she knew. Her passport was confiscated. She was in a prison cell, and the only concession she'd received so far was that a message would be sent to Jeni, her only contact in Lima.

It had been frightening enough being alone in the South American jungle, but this was a different kind of fear. There were so many news stories of travellers, including innocent ones, held for years in gaol without a trial. Her baby might be born in prison! But it wasn't just the imprisonment. Rylla knew, in her heart of hearts, she was still far from well. If she hadn't been in such a hurry to get out of Peru and avoid seeing Jacques again she would still have been in hospital.

Next day, a scared-looking Jeni arrived.

'Why have they put you in prison, Rylla? No one would tell me anything. I've organised a message for Irving, but heaven knows when he'll get it.'

Until now Rylla had managed to keep a tight grip on her emotions. She hadn't even shed tears in private. But having a friendly sympathtic ear into which to pour her troubles set her lips trembling as she explained. Jeni was incredulous.

'But *you* wouldn't do a thing like that. I haven't known you long. But I'd be prepared to swear you're as honest as Irving himself.'

The older woman was even more aghast when Rylla confided her suspicions about Andy.

'Your own brother!'

'But I could be doing him an injustice. So you mustn't tell anyone, Jeni. Promise?'

'But you can't take the blame for something he's done. Anyway, Irving won't believe it was you. He's bound to guess it was Andy. We've got to get you out of here, Rylla. This is no place for a woman.' She shuddered as she looked around the dismal cell. 'I'd go mad, shut up in a place like this.'

'I'm rather afraid *I* might,' Rylla admitted with a quiver in her voice.

The next week was the most unpleasant Rylla had ever spent. On the eighth day, her cell door was thrown open. Rapidly spoken words and a gesture indicated that she should follow the guard. She was led into a dismal interview room and told she had a visitor.

Expecting to see Jeni again, she was totally unprepared for the sight of the tall figure. For a moment, she stared disbelievingly.

'Jacques! Oh, Jacques!' She forgot everything except the fact that his was a familiar face. For the moment it didn't matter how he had hurt her. He represented hope. A sob, two stumbling steps and she was in his arms.

'Rylla, *ma chère, ma pauvre!*' He held her closely for a moment. 'Thank God I came back to Lima earlier than I'd intended. Irving will be gone at least a month. Jeni's told me everything. Don't worry, *chèrie.* We are going to get you out of here.'

'Jacques, you *do* believe I didn't steal the idol?'

'I *know* you did not!'

'But *they* don't believe me.'

'Leave everything to me, *ma chère.* Trust me, hmm? It may take a day or two.'

At the thought of more time spent in this place, Rylla groaned and sagged against him. Jacques held her more tightly.

'I wish I could take you out of here with me right now. I hate to see you like this.' He began to cover her face with small, passionate kisses. 'Rylla, *je t'aime. Mon Dieu, comme je t'aime!* But do not be afraid. Soon, very soon we shall be together for always.' If only that were true. Rylla bit hard on her lip as, reluctantly, he put her away from him. 'The sooner I am gone, the sooner it will be accomplished. Have courage, *chérie!*'

Somehow she managed to control herself until she was back in her cell. But alone again she lost control. Strangely, she didn't doubt that Jacques could get her out of this mess. It was his words that had upset her. 'Soon we shall be together for always.' She should have told him then that she knew he'd lied. But she hadn't the courage. Not when she needed his help.

Two days passed. Two, three, and even the hope she'd placed in Jacques faded.

'You will come with me, *señorita*!' She had never seen this man before. His English was impeccable, with just the slightest trace of accent.

'Where are we going?'

'You are being released, *señorita*.'

'You mean . . .?'

'We know of your innocence, *señorita*, yes. But the *señor* has not escaped without a severe reprimand for his folly.'

'The *señor*? My brother?'

'The *señorita's* brother?' Rylla didn't like the tone of his laughter. 'You English are so proper. We of Spanish blood understand romance. The *señor* acted unwisely, but,' he leered at Rylla, 'I can understand his foolishness.'

He was talking in riddles. What on earth had Andy told him? As they mounted the stairs from the cells, her companion went on volubly.

'The French are romantics, too. Such originality! For Señor Fresnay to place a valuable artefact in your luggage, ensuring you would be unable to leave Peru after your lovers' tiff.'

Rylla's step faltered. He was talking about Jacques, not Andy. Jacques had put the cat god in her camera case! No wonder he'd been so certain of her innocence. These last few harrowing days had been all his fault. She could scarcely believe him capable of such reckless, dangerous behaviour! He couldn't have been certain of securing her release. She could have rotted here for years. Why had he done it? He couldn't have known she would try to leave Peru without seeing him. Unless . . . unless he'd read her father's letter.

In the outer office, Jacques started forward to greet her. He halted as he met a frosty stare and saw the unsmiling set of her mouth.

'Rylla? Are you unwell? Have you been harmed?'

'Yes, I have! By you!' She swept past him out of the door and she would have continued to walk away, ignoring the waiting chauffeur-driven car. But Jacques caught her arm and thrust her into the vehicle. He gave the address of the hotel then turned to look at her, his own expression grim.

'What is this all about, Rylla?'

'As if you didn't know!' she hissed at him.

For a moment she could have sworn he *didn't* know what she was talking about. Then his face hardened and he sat back on the seat, arms folded, features set.

'Well?' she demanded. 'No explanations? Or should I say lies?'

'There is nothing I wish to say to you at the moment,' he told her. 'This is not the place to say and do to you what I wish.' It sounded like a threat. She shrugged. What greater harm could he do than he'd done already?

The car stopped outside the hotel. By the time Jacques had exchanged a few brief words with the chauffeur, Rylla was waiting impatiently for the lift. Before it came, Jacques was at her elbow. Deliberately, she ignored him as the elevator glided smoothly upward. She made for the door of the familiar suite in the same stubborn silence. Jacques produced a key.

Inside the apartment he grasped her arm and turned her to face him.

'*Now* we will talk, *ma chère*, Rylla,' he told her grimly.

'I've nothing to say to you.' Brown eyes glared into blue.

'*Non?*' He raised an eyebrow. 'I had expected *some* gratitude for getting you out of that place.'

'Gratitude? When it was you got me put there?'

'*Comment?*' He led her over to a sofa and made her sit down. 'Suppose,' he suggested, 'you begin at the beginning, and tell me what I am supposed to have done?'

If she were to begin at the beginning, the list of his crimes would be lengthy. Instead, she said, '*You* put that idol in my camera case. Even though you knew what could happen to me when I went through Customs.'

'Ah!' He actually sounded amused. 'Now I see!'

'In that case,' she snapped, 'you should know it's no laughing matter.'

'*Ma chère!*' He tried to pull her to him, but she fended him off. '*Ma chère*, you cannot believe I would do anything so reckless? That I would do anything to harm you? Why should I?'

'That man said you did it to stop me leaving Peru.'

'Rylla, the only way I could get you out of that place was to offer a substantial bribe. But I doubt if that would have worked without my convincing performance. I told a tarradiddle of a misunderstanding, a broken romance, of my desperation to detain you until a reconciliation could be achieved. Rylla, I am neither a thief nor a fool. I did *not* place the cat god in your luggage. I suspect your brother was responsible for that. But would you have preferred me to accuse Andrew and have him replace you in that cell? Or do what I did? I wove a fantasy that harmed no one except myself, it seems.'

It made sense, she conceded reluctantly. His indignation rang true. But he *had* lied to her about something else.

'Rylla?'

'Yes.' She sighed. 'Yes, I believe you, about that, anyway. It's just the sort of trick I'd expect Andy to pull.'

'You believe me, yet something still troubles you? What is it, *ma chère*?'

She shook her head wearily.

'Nothing.' Reaction had set in now. Anger had drained away, leaving total exhaustion and depression. 'I want to see Jeni, then I'm going to shower. I'm tired and I feel filthy. I've been wearing the same clothes all this time.'

'Jeni is not here. She flew to England today. There is no one here but ourselves.'

'In that case,' she told him icily, 'I'd prefer it if you moved out, too.'

'Move out?'

'Jacques, I'm very grateful to you for getting me out of that awful place and for not involving Andy, but . . .'

'He will be severely reprimanded, nevertheless. He may even lose his position with Irving. But let us not speak of that. Let us speak of you and me.'

'There isn't any you and me.'

'*Pourquoi?*' he demanded. 'You love me. You do?' as she shook her head vehemently. 'You have given me proof of this. And I wish to . . .'

'Don't say it, Jacques! Don't lie to me again. You see, I know about your wife.'

'You know what about my wife?' He didn't even sound dismayed, as a guilty man ought to.

'I know that you're married. That's enough, surely?'

'How do you know this untruth?'

'Because it isn't untrue. You have a rich wife who finances your expeditions. My father said so in his letter.'

He was looking at her rather curiously.

'Then why did you allow me to make love to you?'

'Because I hadn't read the letter then. I only found it later.' She stood up and began to move towards the bedroom door. He rose and followed her.

'Rylla, listen to me. I am *not* married. Your father's information was out of date. It is true, I was married once. And it is true, Colette was a rich woman and while she lived she did invest in my work. But she is dead and her money has reverted to her family. When I told you I was not rich, I spoke the truth.'

'Oh!' Hope flared in her. 'When—when did she die?'

'A year ago.' The blue eyes were suddenly bleak. 'Your brother observed that my name had not been in the news media for some while. That was during Colette's final illness.'

'Did . . .?' Rylla swallowed. 'Did you love her very much?'

'Yes! Why? Would you rather I had married her for her money? That would be in keeping with your family's general opinion of me!'

'Oh, Jacques!' Rylla put a hand on his arm. 'Of course not! I'm sorry, truly I am. Will you tell me about her? What was she like?'

'She was *petite*,' Jacques said soberly, 'fair haired, very slender, much like Jeni.'

'And very unlike me.'

'*Chérie*, I loved Colette, of course I did. She was unique, as *you* are unique. Rylla, it *is* possible to love more than once.'

'But why didn't you tell me you'd been married before? You told me other things, about your parents, about your home.'

'Because, *peut-être*,' he sighed, 'I was still trying to forget. Not Colette, but the pain of losing her. But tell me, Rylla, was it so wrong to wish for happiness again—with you?'

'No! Oh, no!' she assured him a little tearfully. 'But tell me some more about Colette. I want to know. Otherwise her ghost will always be there between us.'

He gathered her into his arms and rested his cheek against her hair.

'*Non,*' he said reassuringly. 'Not between us. Colette would not have wished me to remain lonely. She herself urged that I should remarry when I felt the time had come.'

'She *knew* she was dying?'

'She knew it must happen some day, but not when. She developed multiple sclerosis three years after we were married. But the time we had together was good.'

'You never had any children?'

'No. That has always been a sorrow to me. I have always envied my sister her children.'

This was not the moment to tell him. For a little while longer, she would hug her secret to herself. But not for long.

'And she didn't mind you leaving her when you went on expeditions?'

'She was fascinated by my work. She urged me

to go on with it, even though it took me from her. But when I knew the end was near I would not go. After she died——' Rylla felt him shrug '—for a while I went nowhere. And then Irving contacted me and I felt it was meant. The time had come to put away my sorrow and begin to live again. And then I met you.' He looked down into her face. 'And then I met you,' he murmured.

'And you fell in love with me? When?' She wanted to know the exact moment.

'Not immediately, perhaps,' he disappointed her by saying. 'At first, I was intrigued because you did not seem to share your brother's hostility. Or if you did you were better at concealing it. Then I began to know you, your integrity, the warmth of your nature. Ah, Rylla, who can say where love begins? There is no precise instant of time, no warning, just a sudden sure knowledge.' Throatily, he added, 'And there is desire.'

'So, if I hadn't been detained in Peru, you *would* have tried to see me again?'

'Never doubt it. I suppose,' his face creased in wry amusement, 'we should be grateful to your brother for saving me a long journey, for saving us from many lonely hours apart.' His body was suddenly ardent against hers. 'I want you, *ma chère. Now!* Tell me *you* want *me*?'

She was blushing.

'Yes,' she whispered. 'But I feel so tainted by that wretched cell. At least let me shower and put on clean clothes.'

'*Mais oui!* But,' wickedly, 'let us not bother with the clothes! But by all means let us shower.'

'You mean . . . both of us? Together?'

'Why not?' He was laughing at her tenderly. 'Can you not imagine making love in the shower, *ma chère*?'

Suddenly desperately shy, she shook her head and he bent to kiss her, then lifted her in his arms and carried her. He insisted on undressing her, and made her do the same for him. Then gently he soaped her body, every movement a caress, until she felt she would explode with the intensity of unfulfilled desire. It was an excitingly erotic task to wash his body, a task that increased their mutual arousal until, with sudden urgency, he drew her tightly against him. His fingers pressed into the softness of her buttocks as he held her against the almost painful hardness of his masculinity and she felt his throbbing desire.

'The time for play is over,' he growled against her mouth, as he lifted her, her silky wet body sliding over his in a way that made her gasp.

It was very different to the first time. That had been a feverish coming together. This time it was a slow, reverent worshipping of each other's bodies, until urgency rose to such a pitch it could no longer be contained or denied.

'Do you still wish to keep our love a secret from your father?' he asked her much later.

'No. Somehow I think he'll understand. I'll fly

home as soon as possible and I'll *make* him understand.'

'We will make him understand together,' Jacques said firmly. 'I am not letting you out of my sight until we're safely married. Shall you wish, *chérie*, to go on with your work?'

'As long as I'm able to.'

'Able to?' he queried, and then she told him. For a moment he lay in stunned silence.

'You are carrying my child?'

'Aren't you pleased?' she said diffidently.

'Please! Oh, *ma chère*! I am ecstatic. But *you* do not mind?'

'Not a bit,' she said softly. 'I'm so pleased, so happy.' With her lips, her body, she gave him convincing proof of her pleasure.

'And you will not mind that bearing my children keeps you from travelling with me?'

'I shall mind, but just so long as you come back to me!'

'Always! And remember, whatever I am doing, wherever I may travel, you are always in my heart. *Je t'aime, ma chère* Rylla, *je t'aime*. Never forget that, until the end of the road.'

'Until the end of the road,' she promised him.

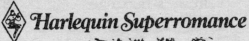

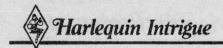

Harlequin Intrigue

Two exciting new stories each month.

Each title mixes a contemporary, sophisticated romance with the surprising twists and turns of a puzzler...romance with "something more."

Because romance can be quite an adventure.

Intrg-1

Romance, Suspense and Adventure

Harlequin Romance

Coming Next Month

Available in October wherever paperback books are sold, or through Harlequin Reader Service:

In the U.S.	In Canada
901 Fuhrmann Blvd.	P.O. Box 603
P.O. Box 1397	Fort Erie, Ontario
Buffalo, N.Y. 14240-1397	L2A 5X3

Temptation™

TEMPTATION WILL BE
EVEN HARDER TO RESIST...

In September, Temptation is presenting a sophisticated new
face to the world. A fresh look that truly brings Harlequin's
most intimate romances into focus.

What's more, all-time favorite authors Barbara Delinsky, Rita
Clay Estrada, Jayne Ann Krentz and Vicki Lewis Thompson
will join forces to help us celebrate. The result? A very special
quartet of Temptations...

- **Four striking covers**
- **Four stellar authors**
- **Four sensual love stories**
- **Four variations on one spellbinding theme**

All in one great month! Give in to Temptation in September.

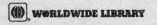

ATTRACTIVE, SPACE SAVING BOOK RACK

Display your most prized novels on this handsome and sturdy book rack. The hand-rubbed walnut finish will blend into your library decor with quiet elegance, providing a practical organizer for your favorite hard-or softcovered books.

Only $9.95

Approximately 16" x 8" when assembled

Assembles in seconds!

To order, rush your name, address and zip code, along with a check or money order for $10.70* ($9.95 plus 75¢ postage and handling) payable to *Harlequin Reader Service*:

Harlequin Reader Service
Book Rack Offer
901 Fuhrmann Blvd.
P.O. Box 1396
Buffalo, NY 14269-1396

Offer not available in Canada.

BKR-1A

*New York and Iowa residents add appropriate sales tax.

HARLEQUIN SIGNATURE EDITION

VIOLET WINSPEAR

HOUSE OF STORMS

Editorial secretary Debra Hartway travels to the Salvador family's rugged Cornish island home to work on Jack Salvador's latest book. Disturbing questions hang in the troubled air over Lovelis Island. What or who had caused the tragic death of Jack's young wife? Why did Jack stay away from the home and, more especially, the baby son he loved so well? And—why should Rodare, Jack's brother, who had proved himself a man of the highest integrity, constantly invade Debra's thoughts with such passionate, dark desires...?

Violet Winspear, who has written more than 65 romance novels translated worldwide into 18 languages, is one of Harlequin's best-loved and bestselling authors. HOUSE OF STORMS, her second title in the Harlequin Signature Edition program, is a full-length novel rich in romantic tradition and intriguingly spiced with an atmosphere of danger and mystery.

Watch for HOUSE OF STORMS—coming in October!

HOFS-1